MR. ICE GUY

A SMALL TOWN SINGLE DAD ROMANCE

SVEN'S BEARD
BOOK TWO

BRENDA ROTHERT

Copyright © 2023 by Brenda Rothert

All rights reserved.

No part of this book may be reproduced in any form or by any electronic or mechanical means, including information storage and retrieval systems, without written permission from the author, except for the use of brief quotations in a book review.

Cover illustration and design by March Illustrations and Kari March Design

❀ Created with Vellum

CHAPTER ONE

Holt

"Was his beard really that long?" my son Spencer asked as he stared up at the massive statue of Sven Karlsson.

"Longer. It went all the way to his feet."

Spencer narrowed his eyes skeptically. He was nine—old enough to know his dad was sometimes full of shit but still never entirely sure of when. I doubted Sven's beard had ever been that long, but it was part of the legend, and as someone born and raised in the Beard, I knew better than to mess with the legend.

My six-year-old daughter Marley tentatively reached her fingertips up toward the flowing beard of the massive Viking statue.

"It brings good luck if you touch it?" she asked, looking to me for confirmation.

"Yep. That's why the finish is all worn away on his beard. Because so many people have rubbed it for good luck."

"I want good luck," she said softly, brushing her hand over the statue's beard.

If anyone deserved some luck on their side, it was my kids. Their lives had been upended in the past few months. Moving from Minneapolis to my small northern Minnesota hometown of Sven's Beard would be a fresh start for all three of us.

It was May, and colorful flowers filled concrete planters and spilled out of wire planters on the decorative black light poles that lined Main Street. Some of the stores and restaurants I'd seen when we pulled into town ten minutes ago were familiar, and others were new to me.

I hadn't come back to the Beard much in the last fourteen years. After being drafted right out of high school to play pro hockey, this place felt too small-time. When I found myself unexpectedly retiring at age thirty-two to raise my two kids on my own, though, I knew there was no better place.

This was home to me. And I hoped it would soon feel like home to my kids, too.

"Daddy, can I have a grilled cheese?" Marley asked me.

"Sure, peanut. We'll go to The Corner Café and get some lunch."

The movers were on their way, but we'd gotten here before them, so it was a perfect time to take a break before they got here. For now, they'd just be moving our stuff into storage, anyway.

"I want to go see our house first," Spencer said.

"We'll eat, go see Grandma and Grandpa and then go see the house."

"Dad!" Spencer gave me an imploring look. "You said we could go see the house."

"And we will."

"I want to see my room."

I ruffled his sandy brown hair. "It's just plywood right now, kiddo. We'll be living at The Sleepy Moose for a few months, remember?"

"I still want to see it."

"You just saw the house three weeks ago," I told Spence. "It hasn't changed much. We'll go see it later."

"Look!" Marley cried, pointing across the street. "What's that place, Daddy?"

She was gaping at a neat little white building with a walkway that looked like it was made of gold brick. The big display windows in the front show-cased cupcakes and chocolates on tiered glass dishes.

"Sweets of Gold," I said. "Looks like a little candy shop."

"Let's go, Mar!" Spence took his younger sister's hand and ran to the edge of the sidewalk, where he paused to make sure there were no cars coming, telling Marley to remember to look both ways.

"Hey!" I called to them, checking to make sure there were no cars coming as they ran across the street to the little shop.

I shook my head and sighed. I couldn't make up for all the time I'd missed in their younger years when I was focused primarily on hockey for nine months of every year. But I'd assumed when I became a single dad recently that at ages six and nine, they'd be good at listening and following directions.

I'd been wrong.

I followed my children to the little shop, where even the doorknob was gold. As soon as I walked in, the smell of baking chocolate chip cookies made my stomach rumble.

"That's fairy dust," an older white-haired man said. "The fairies fly in here at night and sprinkle their magic gold dust on everything."

"Whoa," Marley said, her eyes wide with wonder.

Both of my kids were about to put something in their mouths, and I raced over and snatched whatever it was out of Spencer's hand.

"You can't just eat random stuff strangers give you!" I scolded. "You have an allergy."

"Oh, that's my fault," the older man said. "I'm so sorry. I gave them the truffles and I didn't ask about allergies."

"Mmm," Marley said. "I can taste the fairy dust. It's delicious."

Spencer pushed up his glasses and glared at me. "I can have chocolate, Dad. There's no shellfish in chocolate."

"No, there's no fish anywhere in here," the man said. "Unless chocolate-covered Swedish Fish count, I suppose." He held his hand out to me. "I'm Simon Carmichael. My daughter Olivia owns this store. I'm just here covering it while she gets a haircut. And I apologize again for giving your children something without asking you. When I see those wide eyes, I get a bit ahead of myself."

He seemed like a nice guy. I shook his hand.

"No harm done. I'm Holt Sellers."

His eyes lit up. "Holt Sellers? Our hometown hockey star?"

"Dad." Spencer tugged on my shirt. "Can I have my truffle back?"

I passed him the candy and returned my attention to Simon. "I'm retired now."

Simon nodded with approval. "You went out while you were still on top. Smart man."

I went out because my life imploded out of nowhere, but I wasn't about to correct him. Fourteen years of pro hockey was a good run, and I planned to be very involved in youth hockey in the Beard.

"Spencer, look!" Marley cried as she looked at a display case of cupcakes. "The fairies dusted all of them."

"Can we get cupcakes, Dad?" Spencer asked.

"You haven't had lunch yet."

Marley looked back at me with a toothless smile. "Can I have a chocolate one? Please?"

Mealtimes were a struggle with my kids. I couldn't cook, but I still wanted them to eat healthy food. They'd voted down all my efforts at steamed chicken, shrimp and vegetables in different combinations. All they wanted was macaroni and cheese, grilled cheese and sweets.

"We'll get some for later," I said. "But you have to eat some vegetables at lunch."

"Vegetables are gross," Spencer complained.

Simon grinned. "How many cupcakes would you like?"

"Ninety-nine," Marley said, not missing a beat.

"Um, *no*," I said, giving her a look. "We're not getting ninety-nine cupcakes."

"Why not? It's less than a hundred," she said.

I shook my head and met Simon's gaze. "We'll take four."

"Four?" Spencer looked downright offended by my order. "Who gets the extra one? I should get it because I'm the oldest."

"One for each of you and one each for Grandma and Grandpa," I said. "Pick out what kind you want."

"Chocolate," Marley said immediately.

"I was going to pick that one!" Spencer cried.

Simon's eyes sparkled with amusement as he said, "We have lots of chocolate cupcakes, you can both get that kind."

"I don't want the same as her," Spencer said, glowering. "She's a copycat."

"Hey guys?" I said, my blood pressure rising. "Am I wearing a black-and-white-striped shirt right now?"

Spencer took in my gray T-shirt and gave me a puzzled look. "No."

I looked at my daughter. "Do I have a whistle around my neck?"

She gazed up at me, inspecting the area. "No, Daddy."

"Right." I pointed at the two of them. "Because I'm not a referee. You can each pick out the kind of cupcake you want *now*, with no more arguing, or we're leaving without any cupcakes."

"I'll take Oreo," Spencer said immediately.

"Oh, I want Oreo too!" Marley said.

I glanced at Spencer, who was scowling and pressing his lips together. He was trying so hard to remain silent that I almost laughed.

"Good choice," Simon said. "And what about the grandparents?"

"Vanilla for both of them," I said.

"What about you, Daddy?" Marley asked. "Don't you want one?"

I shook my head. "I try not to eat much sugar, peanut."

"But you're retired now, Dad," Spencer said. "Might as well let yourself go."

I sighed heavily. I'd never imagined myself retiring at age thirty-two when I wasn't even injured. Unless my ego counted. My ex-wife Andrea had done quite a number on that.

Simon passed me a box of cupcakes and said, "Let me just ring that up."

The sign on the bakery case said the cupcakes were four dollars each, so I passed him thirty dollars in cash and said, "Keep the change. Thanks."

"Thank you," he said, smiling. "And welcome home."

———

"STOP WITH THAT NONSENSE," my mom said later that afternoon. "You'll stay with us, of course."

I'd known this was coming. My younger sister Kelsey, who was twenty-six, was still studying to become a pediatrician. She was a long way from being ready to have kids, and she was my only sibling. So my parents were crazy excited about me moving home, and they wanted me and the kids to stay at their house until our house was finished.

Nope. I'd booked a two-bedroom suite at The Sleepy Moose before I broke ground on the house, knowing we'd be moving here as soon as the kids finished school. I loved my parents, but the small three-bedroom ranch I'd grown up in was too small for five people to live in comfortably.

"We're already booked at The Sleepy Moose," I said. "And trust me, you'll see us all the time."

"Can you believe this?" Mom asked Dad. "We hardly see our grandchildren all these years and now he won't even let them stay in our home?"

Dad looked back and forth between me and

Mom, trying to decide who to piss off. I jumped in to save him from choosing.

"The kids can spend the night here anytime," I said.

"I want to spend the night!" Marley said.

Mom beamed at her. "Grandma will make you pancakes and sausage in the morning, honey. I have games for us to play and I bought some DVDs for movie nights."

"DVDs?" I cringed. "Ma, the nineties called and they want their entertainment back."

"I like DVDs because then we can watch movies as many times as we want."

I furrowed my brow and looked at my dad. "You know you can do that with streaming services too, right?"

Mom responded before he could. "No more lip from you, mister. I made biscuits and gravy. Come sit down at eat."

I sighed heavily. We'd eaten lunch at The Corner Café, but there was no use arguing with my mom. Now that I'd moved home, she'd make it her mission to put a couple of inches on my waist with her home cooking.

I wasn't planning to let myself go, but I also couldn't say no to Mom's homemade biscuits and gravy.

As I pulled a chair up to the round oak table I'd eaten meals at with my family as a kid, I knew I'd made the right decision coming back. Mom fussed over the kids washing their hands, which I never remembered to do.

Andrea had always taken care of the kids. I focused on hockey. But now that it was just me, Spencer, and Marley, we were finding our own way. It wasn't easy, but it was always worth it.

CHAPTER TWO

Shea

"Right behind you with...ow, ow, ow....hot!" Nina yelled.

"Where are my eggs?" I asked as I whisked a fresh batch of hollandaise sauce. "Please tell me these aren't my eggs."

Someone had plated eggs benedict with poached eggs that looked like they'd been through a war zone. The whites were an uneven mess. I glared at Darren, the newest cook at The Sleepy Moose.

"You didn't turn the water down, did you?"

"You can't cook eggs unless the water is hot," he countered.

"Right, but like I told you, you have to bring it to a rolling boil but turn it down right before you add the eggs to avoid turbulence. We can't use any of these."

He scoffed. "They taste the same, and you're covering them in sauce anyway."

I'd have to deal with him later. We had thirteen guests waiting on eggs benedict, and my sauce wouldn't last much longer.

"Nina, make me thirteen poached eggs," I said. "Darren, get rid of these."

"Whatever you say, boss," he muttered.

He was so fired. Not only had I told him how to make poached eggs many times, I'd even written it down, and he still refused to follow my directions.

We were at the beginning of our busiest season, summer, and there was a reason The Sleepy Moose was filled to capacity. We never compromised on quality and service, no matter how busy we were. I'd been the head chef here for four years, and I had no tolerance for second-rate cooks.

As I whisked, I watched Priscilla, another one of our cooks, carefully arrange fresh berries on top of mascarpone toast. It was a trademark breakfast dish here at The Moose, one I was particularly proud of.

"Good," I said. "Did you try any of the berries we got in yesterday?"

"I did. The raspberries and blueberries are good,

but the blackberries are a little bitter, so I had to add some sugar."

I groaned. "Steve swore they'd be ripe after I complained last time. I think it's time to look for a new berry distributor."

"Where's the coffee?"

Natalie, who managed the waitstaff at The Moose, was in the process of glaring individually at the kitchen staff when I walked over to her.

"Nat, the coffee is *your job*," I reminded her.

"I told you I'm covering as a server this week. I'm down two people. I can't wait tables and keep up with the coffee."

She was good at organizing the staff, but no one liked Natalie because she was so...Natalie.

"Just because you said you wanted us to do something doesn't mean we agreed to do it," I said. "Now get out, we're swamped."

She huffed and grabbed a bag of coffee grounds, tearing it open. "You're swamped? Yeah, so are we, but we have to deal with the complaining customers. And you know what helps a whole lot? Coffee. It's not too much to ask—"

I drowned her out as I walked over to survey the incoming tickets. Every summer morning at The Moose was busy, but the weekends were particularly brutal.

"That gets a mint garnish," I called to a passing server.

"Eggs, Chef," Nina called, plating the perfectly prepared poached eggs.

"Perfect, thank you," I said, still carrying my pan of sauce and whisking it to keep it fresh.

"These have to go out within thirty seconds!" I called as I poured sauce onto each plate. "How much longer on those biscuits?"

"Three minutes, Chef," a summer intern named Marcus said.

"Get the baskets prepped so you can load the biscuits into them as soon as they come out," I said.

"Yes, Chef."

He was a college student, eager to learn everything he could here. During our busy times, I didn't have time to teach anyone, but I always made time after the breakfast and lunch rushes.

"Shea," Natalie called, "The Lord wants to see you."

I groaned inwardly. I didn't have time to chat with Keller Strauss, the ultrarich Beard resident the kitchen and waitstaff here referred to as The Lord. He was treated like a divine presence everywhere he went, but he also poured millions into our little community, so I guessed he deserved it.

Busy or not, when The Lord called, we ran.

"Got this?" I asked Nina.

"Yes, Chef."

She'd been my sous-chef for two years now, and I adored her. Nina wasn't just an excellent chef. She knew all my quirks and was the best support person I could ask for. We weren't just coworkers but friends.

I took off my apron and hung it on a hook near the door before heading out to the huge dining hall. The ceiling was vaulted and covered with cedar planks, and the wall looking out to Lake Karlsson was all windows. It was a sunny day, and light sparkled on the gently lapping waves.

Keller always sat at the same table, and I smiled when I got close and saw who was there with him this morning.

"Who's in charge around here?" my brother Grady asked, looking gruff. "My toast was burned."

"You get what you deserve," I said lightly.

"Hey," my brother's fiancée Avon said, standing up to hug me. "Everything was amazing as usual."

Grady, Avon and Keller all wore casual summer clothes—T-shirts and shorts for Grady and Avon and a polo and shorts for Keller. Keller spent a lot of time here in the summer, but when we were neck-deep in snow during the winter, he often went to one of his homes in a warmer climate.

"The biscuits were especially good today," he said.

"You probably got them within five minutes of them coming out of the oven," I said. "We're down an oven right now, so we cook them nonstop during breakfast."

Keller was in his midforties, and he still had a full head of dark hair. He was known for being particular but also very generous.

"Hey, when are you coming to work for me?" he asked for at least the tenth time. "I'm not sure if you heard, but I pay well."

He wanted to hire me as his private chef, which sounded incredibly boring to me. The kitchen here was sometimes stressful but never boring. I didn't want to cook for just Keller and his cronies, no matter how much he paid me.

"You can eat my cooking here anytime," I said, smiling.

"I'd rather eat it in my dining room. Did you know I just bought a place in the Maldives? My chef travels with me."

Visiting the Maldives was a dream of mine, but not as anyone's personal chef. Fortunately, Grady must have sensed my discomfort because he jumped in to save me.

"We're talking about the new youth hockey

complex. Holt got into town yesterday and we're catching up with him at lunch today."

My stomach somersaulted at the mention of Holt Sellers. I'd heard he was staying here while his new home was being built, but I'd forced myself not to check on the dates he'd booked.

I was a thirty-one-year-old woman—too old for a crush. Hopefully, Holt had lost most of his teeth playing pro hockey, and I was also pulling for a receding hairline. The less attractive he was these days, the better.

"Avon," I said, walking over to my future sister-in-law. "We need to get together soon for some wedding menu planning."

"I trust you," she said with a smile. "But I'll never say no to sampling your cooking."

My brother had found his perfect match in Avon. She was smart, beautiful and, most importantly—strong enough to stand up to Grady when he was being difficult.

"I have an idea for a chocolate cake with raspberry filling," I said. "But I want each of the three tiers of the wedding cake to be a different flavor."

"I love that."

Grady gave me an offended scowl. "Doesn't it matter what kind of cake I want?"

"Not really. Happy wife, happy life."

"Yeah, okay," he said. "Just don't forget I hate coconut cake."

As though I could forget. Grady was very vocal about his likes and dislikes, which was another reason Avon's go-with-the-flow personality complemented his so well.

"And pound cake," he added. "Pound cake is gross."

"We'll save the pounding for the wedding night," I said lightly. "I need to get back to the kitchen, guys."

I waved as I left and headed back in the direction of the kitchen. While walking, I saw a little boy sitting alone at a table, his brow furrowed as he stared at his untouched scrambled eggs, bacon and toast.

"Hey, everything okay?" I asked, stopping at his table.

He looked up at me through wire-rimmed glasses. "Does this have shellfish in it?"

Poor kid. He was probably hungry but worried about eating something he was allergic to.

"There are no shellfish in it," I assured him. "I'm the chef here, and we have a special area in the kitchen for shellfish. None of this food was anywhere near there."

"Okay, thank you," he said.

He was wiry, his sandy brown hair cut short and

his expression serious. Though he was sitting at a table with four chairs, there was nothing on the table but his plate.

"Are you here alone?" I asked him.

"No, my dad's coming. He was here, but he went back to our room to poop because he doesn't like pooping in public bathrooms."

"I see." I held in a laugh. "Well, I'm Shea, and if you need anything else, ask for me and I'll come right out, okay?"

"Okay. My name's Spencer." He set down his fork and offered me his hand.

I shook his hand, impressed by his maturity. "How old are you, Spencer?"

"I'm nine."

"It's very nice to meet you. I hope you enjoy your stay."

"Thank you," he said, biting off the end of a slice of bacon.

I wanted to sit down and talk to him, but the hollandaise sauce wasn't going to whisk itself, so I gave him a little wave and went back to the kitchen.

The kids who stayed here made my job more fun. I hoped to one day have kids of my own, though it was looking less likely with each passing year.

CHAPTER THREE

Holt

"Holt Sellers," Ryan Grady said with a grin. "It's been too long, man."

He gave me a backslapping man hug, and then Keller Strauss did the same. They sat at a table at the bar in The Sleepy Moose, where we were meeting up to discuss the new youth arena.

"How's retirement?" Keller asked me. "Are you getting in lots of fishing?"

I scoffed. "Are you kidding? I'm a single dad. I cut crusts off of PB&Js, run my kids around to activities and fall asleep reading bedtime stories."

"Living the dream," Grady said.

"Aren't you engaged?" I asked him wryly.

"Yep. The wedding is next month."

"Shit, man. This time next year, you'll be walking around with a baby sling."

He shrugged. "I hope so. We want kids. And my mother is so desperate for grandkids, I think she might start overseeing our efforts to get pregnant."

Keller nodded. "Yeah, I can actually see her setting up a lawn chair at the foot of the bed. Maybe wearing one of those hats with a light on it."

I laughed and did my best imitation of a mom. "Son, you need to go deeper!"

Keller cackled and joined in. "No, that's not where her clit is, Ryan!"

Grady grimaced. "Stop it, assholes. I don't need that mental image living rent-free in my head."

Keller and I exchanged a look as a server approached our table. I ordered a light beer, still too full from my late breakfast with Spencer to eat.

"Seriously, though," I said to my old friends, "if you guys know of any six-year-old girls or nine-year-old boys, I want to help my kids make friends here."

"Isn't Mark Hanes's daughter around six?" Grady asked Keller.

"Probably. And the Henson triplets are nine, two of them are boys."

"Maybe I should have a party or something," I

said. "Spencer's turning ten in July. You think they'd let me have a party here?"

"Have it at The Barn," Keller said.

I furrowed my brow, unsure what he meant.

"It's a huge barn-shaped building I had built for events," he said. "It's on the other side of the lake. We do barn dances, bonfires, wedding receptions, that kind of thing."

"That sounds perfect. Andrea always planned the kids' parties, so I'll have to figure all that out."

"Talk to my sister," Grady said. "She's great at event planning. She and Avon are planning the wedding."

"How is Shea? I haven't seen her since high school."

"Shea's good. She's the chef here."

"Really? That's great."

I vaguely remembered Grady's younger sister. We hadn't hung out much since she was younger, but I'd seen her a few times when I was with Grady. I remembered her with braces and thick glasses. Sweet kid.

"So, if you don't mind my asking, is your ex-wife nearby?" Grady asked.

I knew when I chose to move back to my small hometown that my life would be subject to greater scrutiny than it had in Minneapolis. Everyone knew everyone here, and they also thought they should know every*thing*. I considered Grady and Keller friends, so I didn't mind them asking. The rumor mill would churn no matter what.

"She's in California," I said. "She met someone else about a year ago and decided to tell me about it after he got her pregnant."

"No shit?" Keller's eyes widened.

"No shit. She filed for divorce and took me to court, trying to get full custody so she could move the kids to California, where her baby daddy lives, but the judge wouldn't give her permission to move, so she gave me full custody and went by herself."

My friends just stared at me for a few seconds.

"Jesus," Grady finally said. "I'm so sorry, man."

I shrugged. "It hit me hard when it went down, but I'm in a better place with it now. So are the kids. I retired so we could all get a fresh start."

"Do you still have to pay her alimony?" Keller asked.

I chuckled, though I wasn't amused. "Hell yeah, I do. And she got half of everything. But I've been smart with money, so I just paid her and moved on. Honestly, it just felt great to be rid of her."

"Had to be hard on the kids, though," Grady said.

That was an understatement. Marley had cried herself to sleep in my arms for nearly two weeks after her mom left. Spencer was quieter about his feelings, but I'd taken both of them to counseling for six months after Andrea split, and Spencer's counselor had told me he had a lot of big feelings to work through.

"Yeah, it was. But if I'm being honest, Andrea carried most of the parenting load when we were married. It took two weeks of solo parenting for me to see that I had to retire."

"Don't beat yourself up over that," Keller said. "You were a pro athlete and that takes total dedication. Her only responsibility was the kids."

I shrugged. "Yeah, I guess what I mean is that I'd never have known my kids as well as I do now if the divorce hadn't happened."

Grady grinned. "Look at you, all wise and shit. Now we just need to find a nice Beard girl for you."

"No way. After what Andrea did to our kids, I don't want them worrying I'm going to shack up with someone and leave them, too. My kids and the new arena are my entire focus."

"Speaking of the arena," Keller said, "I had my CFO run some numbers based on the sign-ups we have so far, and it looks like we're actually going to make money off of this thing."

Keller and I were fifty-fifty partners in the new youth hockey complex. It was a multimillion-dollar project, and we'd both invested because we were passionate about it, not because we expected to make money on it. I was surprised to hear him say there was even a possibility.

"That's unexpected," I said.

"It'll take a while, of course. But we already have hundreds of players signed up and the place isn't going to be done for another six months."

I nearly choked on my beer.

"Hundreds?"

Keller nodded. "People who have already paid in full for a year just to hold their kids' spots."

"Our current facility is way over capacity," Grady said. "We have people signing up their newborn babies to start peewee hockey when they turn four. We're the only town in a two-hour radius that has a decent program."

Grady and I would be coaching at the new facility, and I couldn't wait to get started. I'd have plenty of time to finish my house and settle in before the arena was done. But I was far from ready to stop working altogether. Since I couldn't fulfill the demanding travel schedule of being a player, I'd be doing the next best thing with coaching.

"Your fiancée doesn't mind you being gone a couple evenings a week?" I asked Grady.

"Not at all. She has to cover city council and

school board meetings some evenings, so I'm planning to coach on those nights. And she likes watching the games."

When Grady and I had played football together, he'd been pretty intense. He took his sports very seriously. I was sure he was the same way as a coach.

"Now that you're here, I need you to take over as project manager on the complex," Keller said. "I've had one of my employees doing it, but she's eager to get back home to New York."

"Sure, I can do that."

"You'll also need to join the business bureau as soon as possible," Grady said, his expression serious. "Join at the gold level, I don't want to hear any bitching about how much it costs."

Keller grinned. "I already did that, Grady, and I'm sure you can count on Holt for the showdown."

I looked between the two of them, confused. "The what?"

"The Summer Showdown," Grady said. "We have one every winter and every summer, and the teams are made up of representatives from the gold-level supporters of the business bureau."

"I think I remember this," I said. "It's the obstacle course thing, right?"

"Yep. I'm taking that trophy back next month."

"I'll help out however I can."

"Just be a beast if you're on my team, and break your foot or something if you get on the other team."

Grady reminded me of one of my teammates in Minneapolis. Intense, but funny as hell.

Since I was starting all over here, I was glad to have friends to return to. Raising two kids on my own, I'd need them.

CHAPTER FOUR

Shea

I was fit to be tied. After making it from my office near the kitchen to the other side of the resort in record time, I stopped Caden Hawke outside the door to his office with just a look.

"Are you okay?" he asked.

"Not really. I just got the notification that you added back-to-back dinners in the private dining room Tuesday night."

He nodded and opened the door to his office. "Why don't we discuss that in here?"

Caden was the resort manager, meaning he was technically my boss. He told me how many people I could hire, but I chose who those people would be. He approved my budgets and requests for equipment, which was usually just a technicality. He also didn't mess with my schedule for events in the private dining hall.

Usually.

As soon as we were both inside and he'd closed the door, I reminded Caden of the conversation we had a few weeks ago.

"Hey, you said you wouldn't add events to the dining schedule without asking me first."

He gave me an apologetic look. "I didn't ask because I knew you'd say no, and these dinners are both nonnegotiable."

I scoffed. "I get that you want to make things happen for guests when they ask, but I can't prep and serve the main dinner plus two others at the same time. I just don't have the manpower."

Caden sat down behind his desk and sighed heavily. "I know, Shea. But one of the dinners is for Steve Hoffman's extended family and the other one is for some bigshot hockey stars Keller is bringing into town."

I groaned, wanting to be mad at my boss but knowing I couldn't have said no to either of those dinners, either. Steve Hoffman had been bringing his family to The Sleepy Moose every summer for more than twenty-five years. And no one in the Beard said no to Keller. It was kind of impossible, given the millions of dollars he infused into our community every year.

"I have no idea who I'll even hire, but can I hire some temporary staff for that night?"

"Of course. Whatever you need."

I sat down in front of Caden's desk, put my hands on my knees and buried my face in my hands. "I need a few clones of myself and about ten of Nina."

"I know this is the last thing you probably want to hear, but the Darby Divas are coming in this afternoon. They'll be disappointed if they don't get their 'tea time.'"

His "tea time" air quotes made me laugh. The Darby Divas had been coming to The Sleepy Moose for a week every summer for more than twenty years. They were five lifelong friends from Darby, Pennsylvania, who were approaching age eighty. And while they loved the tiered trays of pastries and tiny sandwiches the kitchen put together for their afternoon teas, not one of them actually drank tea. Those ladies liked spiked fruity drinks, heavy on the spike.

"Nina's on it," I said. "She made them cucumber sandwiches and cherry pastries for today."

"Excellent."

I sat up straight and took a deep breath. My to-do list was long, and I didn't have time to sit here.

"Hey, Caden?" I said as I stood.

"Hmm?" He was writing something and didn't even look up.

"You said anything I need for next Tuesday, right?"

"Of course."

"Can you come help out in the kitchen that evening?"

He looked up at me, his eyes wide. "What?"

"Yeah, I mean...you know this place really well and if you could serve food, it would free up another set of hands to cook."

He considered. "Just taking the food to tables? That's all?"

"That's all."

"Okay, I can do that."

An idea hit and I immediately realized it would help make next Tuesday evening more manageable.

"I also need Lenny from maintenance for the evening," I said, reaching for the door handle to leave Caden's office.

Caden hummed his disapproval. "Not Lenny. He doesn't know how to make small talk with guests."

"He won't have to," I said as I opened the door. "I just need him to man the outdoor grill. We'll do steak and baked potatoes for Keller's hockey dinner.

And apple pie. I can have all the prep done by midafternoon."

"Love that. Have I told you yet today that you're a genius?"

I smiled at my boss. "Remember that when you get my request for a new Viking oven."

He sighed wearily and shooed me from his office.

I was only a few feet into my trip back to the kitchen when my phone buzzed in my pocket with a text from Francis, the front desk manager at The Sleepy Moose.

Francis: The Bigfoot guys are asking where their dessert is.

Crap. I thought Nina was on that. A statewide Bigfoot enthusiast's club met four times a year in our largest conference room, and they liked their desserts. I'd planned a lighter lunch for them today specifically so we could serve several different sweet treats after the meal.

I power walked back to the kitchen, where Nina gave me a frantic look as soon as she saw me.

"I know," she said. "But the brownies needed to be frosted. You would have said the same thing."

Nina was a thirty-six-year-old mom of two. She'd never been to culinary school, but she was more talented in the kitchen than many trained chefs. I was fortunate to have a right-hand woman who was both an outstanding cook and had a steady head.

"What can I do?" I asked as she poured sugar into a huge mixing bowl.

"Warm some blueberry sauce for the cheesecakes. Eli's taking care of the coffee station in the conference room."

We worked in silence, Nina prepping a big batch of creamy chocolate frosting and topping two huge trays of brownies with it while I warmed enough sauce for two New York–style cheesecakes.

"Priscilla sliced a cheesecake," Nina said as she smoothed out the frosting on a batch of brownies. "She was trying to help. It's in the walk-in. I'm sure we'll go through all of it at dinner."

The Minnesota Bigfoot Research Society Board of Directors was adamant that we not cut their desserts into servings because they said they felt "portion-shamed" when we did. There were fourteen people in the conference room, and they'd demolish every bite of the cheesecakes and brownies.

I put each cheesecake on a simple white pedestal and poured blueberry sauce over them, the sweet smell of the sauce making my stomach rumble.

It was ironic that I worked around delicious food

all day and was lucky if I had time to make a quick ham sandwich for lunch.

Nina loaded the brownies onto the main shelf of a wheeled metal cart and I stacked plates, utensils and napkins on the bottom shelf.

"There's no room for the cheesecakes," she said. "I'll get the other cart."

She returned in a couple of minutes, looking confused. "The cart's not there."

"It's okay, I'll carry them."

She gave me a skeptical look, her brow lowered. "Are you sure?"

"Yep. We have to get these into the Bigfoot guys before they revolt. These pedestals are easy to carry."

We set off, Nina opening the double doors to the kitchen with her back and me carefully keeping them open with my back and easing out. After working in the kitchen for so long, we knew the potential pitfalls.

"Corner!" Nina called out, warning anyone on the other side of the corner that we were approaching with food in hand.

"Did you hear the fishing derby was moved from Monday to Tuesday next week?" Nina asked me.

"What? No."

"Yeah, they haven't called to tell us, but Ted told

me this morning. They're moving it because of Harold Fineman's celebration of life on Monday."

I groaned. "I don't know what we're going to do. We're already booked over capacity on Tuesday evening. We'll be ordering pizza for the dining hall."

Nina laughed. "Guests always come first. Tell the fishing derby no if you have to."

I balked. "Yeah, that'll go over like a lead balloon."

"Well, they should have asked instead of just moving it and expecting us to be able to do it."

This was why Nina was my perfect work sidekick. I had a tendency to say yes to everything, not wanting to disappoint anyone. She was more practical.

"You're right. Can you let Ted know there's no way we can do that? We're maxed out for Tuesday evening, but any other night next week should work. Check the schedule to be sure."

"Sure thing, boss."

My phone buzzed in my pocket and even though I couldn't get it out with a cheesecake in each hand, I knew it was about the ETA of the desserts.

"Let's hurry," I said, picking up my pace and passing Nina and the cart.

I wasn't even aware of what happened next until it was over. I felt a hard thud and a squish, and somehow Nina managed to sweep one of the cheesecakes out of my hand before I fell to the ground.

"Oh no," she said softly.

The thud was me smacking into someone, which knocked the wind out of me. And the squish? That was the cheesecake I'd inadvertently dumped onto his chest.

"Are you okay?" the man asked, scrambling to his feet and crouching down beside me.

Dark hair. Blue eyes. My heart pounded as I stared at Holt Sellers, too dazed for a second to even speak. The boy I'd had a secret crush on as a teen had grown into an even more handsome man, his shoulders wider and his voice deeper. Even the little worry line between his brows made this more mature version of Holt sexier in a way that terrified me.

"Shea?"

My embarrassment skyrocketed at his recognition of me. I'd always felt awkward around Holt, and it didn't get any more awkward than slamming a blueberry-sauce-topped cheesecake into a guy wearing a white shirt and having him show concern for me instead of anger.

"Holt, I'm so sorry. I was in a huge hurry and I didn't look around the corner."

He put a hand out to help me up, but I scrambled

to my feet on my own, too mortified to take his hand. When I got to my feet, he was giving me a look that was a mix of concern and amusement, the corners of his eyes tipping up in a smile even though the worry line was still there.

"I always thought I looked better in blue anyway," he said.

The sound of a little giggle made me turn, and I saw two children standing nearby. One of them was Spencer, the boy I'd already met, and the other was a little girl with long brown curls and Holt's blue eyes.

The girl was laughing while Spencer looked like he wanted to laugh but knew he shouldn't.

"Shawn!" Nina called to a passing bellboy. "Can you get this cart?"

Shawn took over pushing the cart and Nina turned to me.

"I'm going to get this delivered and then I'll come help clean up," she said.

I waved her on and glanced down at my apron, which had blueberry sauce smeared on it. Most of the cheesecake and its sauce had ended up on Holt.

"We'll get your clothes into the laundry right away," I said, the words spilling out of me in a rush. "And if it's ruined, of course, we'll replace it."

"I'm not worried about the shirt. Are you okay?"

Physically, I was fine, but I was definitely not

okay. I didn't know if my heart was racing because I'd made such a fool of myself or because my former crush was three feet away from me, looking like an absolute eleven.

Under normal circumstances, I would have called for maintenance to clean up the mess and continued with the dessert delivery.

But I couldn't. All I could do was stand there and look at him.

I'd woken up this morning a fully functioning adult with a full vocabulary, but Holt Sellers had turned me back into a tongue-tied teenager.

CHAPTER FIVE

Holt

Where was the shy girl with braces and a flat chest? The beautiful woman standing before me looked nothing like Ryan Grady's kid sister. Even covered by an apron, Shea was unmistakably curvy in all the right places, her caramel eyes framed with thick dark lashes.

Thank Christ, no one but me knew her embarrassed flush was making me hot. I hadn't been with a woman in a very long time. Hadn't even thought about being with one until this moment.

"I'm fine," Shea said, smiling. "And again, I'm so sorry. I should have paid closer attention."

A maintenance man tipped his cap at us as he rolled up his mop cart.

"Sorry about this, Lenny," Shea said. "It was entirely my fault."

"It's not a big deal, it's just a deal," he said warmly. "I'll have this cleaned up in a jiff."

We stepped aside so Lenny could work and Shea gave me another apologetic look.

"I'll send someone from housekeeping to pick up your laundry right away," she said.

"Don't worry about it. They're doing all of our laundry anyway. This shirt can wait until the regular laundry day."

"Are you sure?"

Fuck the shirt. This was the first time since Andrea that I'd felt a real attraction to a woman. Something that wasn't just a passing, two-second attraction, anyway. I glanced at Shea's ring finger and was relieved to find it empty.

Checking to see if she was married? What the hell was I thinking? This was Grady's sister and the kids and I had just gotten into town a couple of days ago. My plan was to focus entirely on getting the kids settled here, finishing our new home and building the new arena.

"Yeah," I said, Marley sliding her hand into mine. "Shea, this is my daughter Marley and my son Spencer."

When she smiled, my determination to stick to the plan wavered. Damn, she was beautiful.

"Spencer and I met in the dining hall," she said. "And Marley, it's very nice to meet you."

Marley turned her face toward me, too shy to respond.

"I hear you guys are with us for a while," Shea said.

"Yeah, until our house gets finished. I'm hoping to be in there within six weeks."

"Well, we have lots of fun things going on here in the summer. We do campfires out on the lawn in the evenings, swimming and canoeing in the lake and I teach kids' baking classes."

Spencer looked at me hopefully. "Can I take a baking class, Dad?"

"Yeah, that sounds like a plan."

A blob of blueberry cheesecake fell from my shirt onto the floor, sending the kids into another fit of laughter.

"I'll let you get cleaned up," Shea said. "Will you guys be eating in the dining hall tonight?"

"Not sure yet," I said. "My mom said she's making roast one night this week. I can't remember if it's tonight."

"Well, next time you eat in the dining hall, try the

cheesecake. I think you'll like it when it's on a plate instead of, you know...all over you."

She cringed and gave us a final smile before walking over to Lenny to thank him for cleaning up the mess and then walking away.

"Dad, why are you looking at her back?" Spencer asked.

"I, uh...I wasn't."

"Yes, you were. You were staring at her back. Don't be a creeper."

I glanced at Lenny, who was holding back a smile. Damn kids. They were too smart for their own good sometimes.

A COUPLE OF HOURS LATER, Spencer was chasing Marley up the open front staircase of our future home while I talked to the general contractor, Ray.

"This was worth the holdup," I said as I admired the view through the wall of floor-to-ceiling windows that looked out onto Lake Karlsson.

"I agree. The black is a better fit for such a modern design."

The windows with black casing had been back-ordered, and I'd decided a three-week delay was better than switching windows. Now that they were in, I was confident I'd made the right call.

"What is that?" I asked, squinting as I tried to make out a small shape in the middle of the lake.

Ray took a closer look too. "Oh, that's Tipper. He owns The Corner Café."

"Ah. That explains why everyone calls it Tipper's."

"Yeah, he's determined to win the cardboard boat race this year, so he's been experimenting with different designs."

"A cardboard boat?" My brows shot up in surprise. "That far out in the lake?"

"Oh, he had to swim back in a time or two. See, that's why he tows the little rowboat behind him."

Only in the Beard. This was one of the reasons I'd moved here to raise my kids—so they could get to know people who weren't afraid to fail. It was a lesson I hoped to instill in my youth hockey players, too.

If you never fail, you aren't trying hard enough.

I had that saying taped to my locker for years. With the right mindset, all failures build us into stronger, more resilient people. I knew there was a lesson in my failed marriage somewhere, but it was hard to find it when my kids still cried for their mom sometimes.

"Dad, Spencer scared me!" Marley cried, running down the stairs.

"Spence, leave your sister alone," I said absently.

"She's the one who scared me with her ugly face," he said.

"Hey." I turned to lock eyes with him. "Don't be mean to your sister."

He scowled and headed for the basement. I looked back out at the lake, envisioning a future where I woke up to this view every morning.

Despite my fighting children, this place gave me a sense of peace. The lapping waves and scent of freshly cut wood were part of this place that was just mine, Spencer's and Marley's. There would never be memories of Andrea here.

We'd have birthday parties, Christmas mornings and sleepovers here. This would be a place where my kids were always safe, loved and wanted. I'd never let anyone else into their lives who would leave them. Fail them. Make them feel like they weren't good enough.

"The stone came in for the fireplace," Ray said. "Want to see it?"

"Yeah, I do."

I followed him out to the large three-stall garage, where building materials were stored until they were needed. There was also a separate two-stall garage with a loft on the side of my property, which I planned to make into a workshop.

Andrea's affair had forced me to change. I'd been a self-centered, chirp-serving hockey player who spent a few hours a week with my kids. Now, I was a retired full-time dad planning my future wood-working shop and helping build a youth hockey league.

I loved playing hockey bone-deep, but I was a better version of myself now.

"What do you think?" Ray asked, picking up a gray stone that was the size of a small dinner plate.

"I think I was right," I said, grinning.

We'd worked with a female architect and a female interior designer to plan my home, and the designer had been adamant about putting shiplap on the two-story fireplace in the open great room, but I wanted stone.

Earthy, uneven stones would balance out the smooth hardwood floors, giving the great room a strong, rustic focal point. I didn't want to build the farmhouse-style home the designer kept trying to get me into.

"Fuck shiplap," Ray said, carefully setting the stone down.

"My man." I fist-bumped him in agreement.

"The masons will be here Tuesday to get the fire-place done."

I was looking forward to crackling fires on snowy winter evenings when the lake was frozen over. I'd ice-skated on the lake, and my kids would, too.

Maybe someday I'd have someone curled up beside me on those cold evenings. It wouldn't happen for a while, though, if ever. My kids only had one parent left, and I didn't want them to worry I'd leave them, too.

Hell, celibacy was nothing new to me. Andrea had stopped wanting sex with me a long time before she left me. At least now I knew there wasn't even a hope it would change.

No one had it all, and that was something I'd just have to learn to live without.

CHAPTER SIX

Shea

"Well, I'm sure you made an impression," Nina said, avoiding my gaze. "That's never a bad thing."

It was the afternoon after the cheesecake incident, and she was trying—unsuccessfully—to assure me Holt didn't think I was a hot mess. We were prepping supplies for dinner while other cooks peeled potatoes and shucked corn.

"I made an impression alright," I said, shaking my head.

"Do you remember him from high school? Was he close to your age?"

"Did you add that extra butter to the inventory?" I asked, looking up from my clipboard.

"Yep."

I nodded and made a check mark on my inventory sheet. "Holt is three years older than me and two years younger than Grady. So I knew of him but never really knew him."

"Gotcha. He seems like a really nice guy."

I ignored her because I didn't want the entire kitchen staff listening to this conversation. Nina was on a mission to fix me up with someone, and since she hadn't been successful matchmaking me with any men in the Beard, she always had her eye out for attractive male guests.

"Darren, are you all set for the risotto?" I asked, walking over to the big butcher block island where he was peeling potatoes.

"Yeah," he said.

I wasn't confident in his risotto-making abilities, but I had to assign my best cooks to the dinner main courses.

"Don't stop stirring," I said. "Split it between two pots and stir one with each hand."

"I'm not dumb. I know it takes two hands to stir two pots," he said, offended.

"I didn't mean it that way. And make sure the mushrooms aren't just sliced, but chopped."

He sighed heavily and muttered to the employee next to him. "Is she gonna follow me into the bathroom and tell me how to hold my dick when I take a piss?"

I looked up from my clipboard, taken aback. "Darren, I don't care how you piss as long as you wash your hands when you're done. I do care how you prepare food in *my* kitchen, and if that's a problem for you, there's the door."

The room fell into complete silence as I gestured at the double doors. I wanted to fire him, but I couldn't until I found a replacement.

"It's no problem," he mumbled.

"Shea?"

I turned toward Priscilla, who was standing in front of the kitchen doors, her arm around Spencer.

"You have a visitor," she announced.

I smiled, hiding my slight panic. Hopefully Spencer hadn't just heard me dressing down Darren.

"Hi Shea," Spencer said, grinning. "Can I have cooking lessons?"

He was wearing one of the dark gray aprons sold in The Sleepy Moose's gift shop, our logo embroidered on the chest. I didn't know if it was the apron or his eager expression, but I couldn't turn him down.

"Sure, I'll put you to work," I said. "But it might not be anything exciting since we're preparing for dinner."

"That's okay."

I motioned him over to the sink. "First, I'll show you how we wash our hands."

He listened intently to my instructions, washing his hands all the way up to his elbows. I ran through tonight's menu, trying to think of a job he could safely do.

"Do you want to whip butter?" I asked him.

He nodded eagerly. "Sure."

We served baskets of fluffy, fresh-baked rolls at dinner with a dish of whipped cinnamon butter. I showed Spencer how to add the ingredients to the bowls of several stand mixers and turn them on.

"It's three thirty, Chef," Priscilla called from the island.

That meant it was time to kick things into gear for dinner. I had everyone's assigned jobs written on the job board, but I also usually did a quick predinner meeting.

The servers filtered into the kitchen, and soon, the full kitchen and serving staff were waiting for me to brief them on dinner.

"Okay, everyone," I said. "Specials tonight are steak au poivre with red wine pan sauce, roasted fingerling potatoes and creamed spinach or roasted half chicken with mushroom risotto and roasted asparagus. The dessert special is peach tart with vanilla ice cream and caramel sauce." I looked down at my clipboard. "We're out of carrots, so no glazed carrots." I looked back up, scanning the faces around me. "Remember to speak up if you're falling behind at your station. Go to Nina first and if you can't go to her, find me. We go from plate to table in less than a minute. Any questions?"

"Does that tart have nuts?" a server named Jack asked.

"Our only nut-free desserts are vanilla ice cream with berries and apple dumplings. Everything else is prepared in a space where there are nuts. All allergens for the specials are listed on your cards."

"Thank you, Chef," Jack said.

Caden walked through the double doors to the kitchen, his brow furrowed. "Has anyone seen a little boy? Nine years old, wearing glasses and a white T-shirt?"

Every head in the kitchen turned to Spencer. My eyes widened.

"Thank God," Caden said, opening one of the double doors and calling out. "He's in here!"

"Get to work!" I told everyone as Holt ran through the doors into the kitchen.

I didn't want everyone witnessing my second humiliation in as many days.

"Dammit, Spence!" Holt hugged his son tightly

and then bent down to his level. "I was so worried. You can't just leave like that."

"Sorry, Dad. I thought you'd say no."

I approached Holt with a look of apology. "I'm so sorry. I shouldn't have assumed he told you where he was. That's on me."

Holt shook his head adamantly. "No, it's on him." He gave his son a stern look. "I told you to let me know where you are at all times, and I told you not to come in here and bother Shea while she's working."

"It wasn't a bother at all," I said. "He asked, and he's been very polite and helpful."

Nina tugged on my elbow and when I looked at her, she shook her head almost imperceptibly.

I immediately understood my friend's unspoken message: stop undermining Holt while he's trying to tell his son something important.

Damn. If I wasn't dumping food all over him, I was putting my foot in my mouth. I zipped my lips as Spencer looked up at me, his eyes filled with tears.

"Sorry, Miss...Shea," he said.

"Miss Grady," Holt corrected him.

"Miss Grady."

I wanted to talk to Holt about this in private, but the activity in the kitchen was ramping up, and it wasn't the time or place.

"It's okay, Spencer," I said gently. "I enjoyed having you and I appreciate your help."

He looked away, and I was pretty sure he was embarrassed to be seen crying. My heart broke for him. He was a sweet, earnest boy.

"Will you guys be eating in the dining hall tonight?" I asked Holt.

"We will," he said, putting an arm around his son's shoulder.

He'd noticed Spencer was crying, too. Holt patted his shoulder in a silent gesture of comfort, and my crush on him deepened.

"I'll bring out something special," I said. "And when you guys eat that whipped cinnamon butter, tell Spencer what a great job he did making it."

Spencer smiled up at me and Holt gave me a grateful look.

"We'll look forward to it. Thanks, Shea."

"I'll see you soon, Spencer," I said with a little wave.

They left the kitchen and I only snuck one glance at Holt's broad back, his muscled physique filling out his short-sleeved gray T-shirt.

Nina leaned in close. "Is it hot in here, or is it just him?"

"Both," I whispered, grinning at her.

I couldn't deny it—Holt was incredibly sexy. His

concern for his son, coupled with the image of them walking side by side, Holt towering over his small son with an arm protectively over his shoulder, had done me in.

"Chef, where's the seasoning for the chicken?" someone called out from nearby.

The question brought my feet back down to the ground. Sexy athlete nearby or not, I had to concentrate on dinner.

———

"HI, SHEA."

A few hours later, Spencer smiled brightly at me when I stopped at the table he was eating dinner at with Holt and Marley.

"Hi there," I said, setting the platter I was carrying on the table.

I'd checked with their server to make sure my delivery came at just the right time. They'd ordered dinner and were snacking on rolls with cinnamon butter. Holt had a glass of iced tea and the kids both had water.

"As promised," I said. "These breadsticks are called grissini. I brought some beer cheese dip for them."

Spencer's eyes widened as he looked at the long, skinny breadsticks I'd arranged in three jars.

"Does it have shellfish in it?"

"No shellfish. I promise that while you're here, you won't be served anything with shellfish. We keep cards on each guest so we know about their allergies and their favorite foods. Your server will always have that card."

Holt gave me an appreciative look. "That's a great thing to do."

Marley looked at me shyly. "Does the cheese really have beer in it?"

I laughed and exchanged an amused look with Holt. "Just a little bit for flavor."

"My dad likes beer," she said.

"Good to know," I said.

Holt gave me a sheepish look. "I drink beer on occasion. I'm not that into it."

"Don't hog it, Spencer!" Marley cried.

Spencer had moved the bowl of cheese dip closer to him, and Marley couldn't reach it. I was about to go to the kitchen for another bowl when Holt cut in.

"Guys, we're not fighting over cheese dip. It's going between the two of you, okay?"

"It's really good, Dad. You should try it," Spencer said.

"I'm going to, but I'm minding my manners and

not eating when we're still talking to Shea."

"Oh." Spencer put his breadstick down.

"I have to get back to the kitchen," I said. "Save room for dessert because your server will be bringing out flourless chocolate cake for you later. Both the cake and the grissini are off-menu items that we reserve for our most special guests."

Spencer beamed at me. "Can I help in the kitchen tomorrow?"

"Sure. Can you come by around ten in the morning? We can make cookies."

"Can I, Dad?" Spencer asked.

"I want to come, too," Marley said.

"Are you sure you have time?" Holt asked me.

"Absolutely. And in the afternoon, there's a birdhouse-building workshop for kids on the lawn if you guys have time."

"Sounds like a plan," Holt said. "Thanks, Shea."

God, I liked it when he looked at me like that. Frankly, I liked it when he looked at me in any way. I felt a stab of guilt over my thirstiness because Holt was a newly divorced single dad. He was also a friend of my brother's.

I could spend time with his children, but I had to keep my distance from him. The last thing I wanted was to complicate the life of a man who'd been put through an emotional wringer recently.

CHAPTER SEVEN

Holt

"This is unreal," I said as I looked at the wood-framed walls of the Sven's Beard Youth Hockey Complex. "The snack bar is bigger than the locker room in the old facility."

"They'll still sell the same hot dogs, though," Grady said. "I made sure of that."

I shook my head and nudged him. "Working on a happily married pot belly already? You guys haven't even said your vows yet."

"I never gave a shit about washboard abs. Avon says I have a man-bear bod."

Grady's best friend Coulter snorted with laughter. "That's because you're so hairy, man."

Grady silently flipped him off. Times hadn't

changed; we'd all given each other endless shit when playing sports together growing up.

"Sorry I'm late," Keller said, putting on a hard hat as he approached us. "I was delayed taking off in New York because of a storm."

"We were just giving Holt a tour," Grady said.

"I'm sure he told you we'll still have the same hot dogs," Keller said wryly.

I laughed and nodded. "He mentioned it, yeah."

A man in jeans, work boots, a T-shirt and a hard hat approached us. "Hey, how's it going?"

Keller shook his hand and said, "Holt, this is Frank McMahon. He's the on-site foreman. If you ever have questions, he's the one you want to find. Frank, this is"

Frank reached for my hand. "Shit, man, I know who this is. Holt, I'm a big fan. My nephews and I have followed you your whole career, and now they'll get to be coached by you. It's a real honor."

It was the first time since coming back to the Beard that anyone had recognized me more for my years in hockey than for being a native.

"Honor's mine," I said, shaking his hand. "You guys are doing an incredible job here."

"Thank you. Any questions I can answer for you guys?"

Grady furrowed his brow. "Did you guys get the door issue taken care of for the Zamboni?"

"Yep. That opening will accommodate the biggest Zamboni out there with room to spare."

Keller grins. "I'm planning to drive the Zamboni as much as possible."

It was easy to picture our local billionaire perched on the ice-cleaning machine. No matter where in the world he went or how much money he made, Keller had always thought of the Beard as home. I'd thought he was crazy for that when I was younger, but now I understood.

"I have to get back to the station soon," Grady said, looking at his watch. "I want to go check out the locker rooms."

Frank took us on a quick tour of the facility, which was massive. We saw where the main game ice rink and three other rinks would be, and we saw the framed walls for eight locker rooms, several coaching offices, equipment rooms, meeting rooms and bathrooms.

I felt a stir of excitement. Coaching youth hockey had felt abstract until now. Standing in this dream facility made it real.

Keller gestured to a wall right inside the front doors to the facility. "We commissioned an artist to paint a mural of Sven on that wall. He sent me his drawings and I think it's gonna knock everyone's socks off."

Sven Karlsson was the Viking who had founded our small town way back when. There was a statue of him in the town square that had to be at least eight feet tall, his flowing beard a good luck charm that had been rubbed countless times. No one asked how much of Sven was myth and how much was truth because that would ruin the fun.

"He's working on drawings for a Bigfoot mural for a big wall by the snack bar," Keller said. "I'll send everything out in a group email to keep you guys in the loop."

Grady looked at his watch again. "Shit, I have to go. You guys coming to the thing tonight?"

"Wouldn't miss it," Keller said.

"What thing?" I asked.

"It's a barn dance," Keller said. "At The Barn, the place I told you about. You can bring your kids. It's family friendly."

Grady scoffed. "Yeah, til the Markley brothers get tanked."

"Can confirm," Coulter said. "Robbie Markley urinated in a sink in the women's room at a barn dance last year and it got ugly."

"Ugly?" I asked.

"Lana Baker started wailing on him with her handbag. Some other women joined in."

Grady clarified. "Robbie got his ass beat by a bunch of women, and he deserved it."

"Sounds like it."

"There's usually no urinating in sinks," Keller said. "You should come."

I shrugged. "Sure, I'll be there. My kids are staying the night with my parents tonight and I've got nothing else to do."

"Prime time to find a rebound," Grady said.

I cringed. "No, I'm good. The last thing I need is an entanglement with a woman who lives in the same small town I do."

Keller looked at me like I'd just landed from another planet. "Are you planning to be celibate?"

"For the time being, yeah. Raising two kids is a full-time gig."

He nodded. "I admire you for putting them first."

"I have to run," Grady said. "See you guys tonight."

Everyone said goodbye and I headed for the parking lot, checking my phone on the way. I stopped walking when I saw the text I'd received while inside the complex.

Andrea: I miss you guys. Can you call me?

That was a hard no. My ex had a lot of fucking guts asking me to call her. I hadn't blocked her because we needed to be able to reach one another in case of an emergency.

Anger churned in my gut as I deleted the text. Things were going well here, and I wasn't going to let her stir up drama. She was in the past, and I was focused on the future.

———

By the evening, I'd cooled off over the text from Andrea. I'd taken the kids to my parents' house and was driving my truck to The Barn, which looked like it belonged in an architectural design magazine.

The Barn. Only Keller would pick such a simple name for a place this grand. It was a few miles from The Sleepy Moose, located right on Lake Karlsson. The grounds glowed from string lights and had several little areas with gazebos, benches and landscaping.

I parked and went in, admiring the open two-story building. It had warm wood floors and wood plank walls, wood beams visible above. A band played onstage and people were crowded around a large bar area.

"You made it," Coulter said, approaching me with a shoulder clap. "What are you drinking?"

"I'll walk over to the bar with you," I said. "Where's Grady?"

Coulter scoffed. "On the dance floor with his woman. She loves to dance. Grady would walk through fire for that girl, I'm tellin' ya."

I spotted them—Grady was so tall and broad he was hard to miss in a crowd. He and Avon were dancing close, their foreheads resting together. I was happy he'd found someone he loved so much. Andrea and I had never been that way. She was practical and thought sweet gestures were cheesy, so I gave up on them early in the relationship.

"Holt Sellers! Welcome home!" A man clapped me on the back as soon as I reached the bar. "You may not remember me. I'm Ron Markley. I was a few years ahead of you in school."

I didn't remember him at all. But I did remember his last name from my conversation earlier today.

"Hey, thanks, man," I said. "It's good to be back."

"Shots!" Ron called out. "Fireball shots all around! Where's my brother?"

I cringed at Coulter and spoke in a low tone. "I'd rather do a shot of horse piss than Fireball."

"Yep, same. I'm sticking with my beer."

I ordered a Guinness and was standing off to the side of the large dance floor talking to Coulter when Grady and Avon approached us, hand in hand.

"Glad you made it," Grady said.

"I spent the afternoon making birdhouses with my kids. It's nice to have some adult company for a change."

"Damn," Avon said. "I meant to come take photos of that for the paper, but I couldn't get away from the office."

"You didn't miss much. I tried to paint a mammoth on mine, but it looked more like a Rorschach test."

Coulter squinted. "A what?"

"You know, the inkblots that aren't really anything, but they ask people what they think they look like as a psychological test," Avon said.

"Oh yeah, I always see boobs," Coulter said.

Grady nodded. "That is not even a little bit surprising."

Coulter shrugged. "It's no secret I'm a boob man."

"In more ways than one," Grady quipped.

I was about to take a sip of my beer when I saw her and paused everything, including breathing. Shea had just walked into The Barn, and I wasn't the only man who'd noticed.

I'd only seen her with her hair pulled back, and tonight it was loose around her shoulders. She wore a T-shirt that said "Letterkenny Irish," cutoff jean shorts and cowboy boots. I couldn't take my eyes off of her.

Someone stopped her to say hi, putting his hand on her arm, and a flare of jealousy shot through me. What was with me?

She gave him a dazzling smile, said a few words to him, and then walked over to our group.

"Hey, guys," she said, hugging Avon. "Hi Holt, it's good to see you here."

"Yeah, it's nice to be out with adults."

I couldn't think of anything new or remotely entertaining to say. My gaze kept drifting to her bare legs and I had to check myself, forcing my eyes to Grady instead.

"Holt, you remember my sister Shea, right?" Grady said. "She's *my sister*."

His emphasis let me know he'd seen me staring. Grady had always been overprotective of Shea.

"Of course I remember Shea. She's been letting my son bug her at work and he's crazy about her."

She turned her megawatt smile on me and I felt a stirring in my chest. What was it about her that I couldn't look away from?

It was everything. She was beautiful but also

funny and sweet. I'd never seen a woman be so nurturing to my children and damn if it didn't make her irresistible to me. Spencer hadn't been excited about much of anything since his mom left, and Shea had brought back his enthusiasm.

"How did your birdhouses turn out?" she asked me.

"Marley painted hers purple with a rainbow roof. It turned out great. Spence tried to blend colors together, so his is gray, and mine...well, it won't be winning any birdhouse awards."

"It has boobs on it, though," Coulter said.

I shook my head as Shea gave me an alarmed look. "No, it doesn't."

"I need another beer," Coulter said. "Anybody want a drink?"

Everyone passed, and as soon as he was gone, Avon smiled up at Grady. "Want to dance?"

"Absolutely."

They headed back to the dance floor, leaving Shea and me alone. Our eyes met and we both smiled and looked away. I felt like a nervous high school kid at a homecoming dance.

"Hey, thanks for baking cookies with the kids today," I said. "They were really excited to give cookies to their grandparents."

"I loved it. They're really great kids, Holt. You've

done a great job with them."

It wasn't the time or the place to tell her I'd been too busy with hockey to be much of a dad until a year ago. So, instead, I said the only thing that came to mind.

"We could dance. If you want to, I mean."

CHAPTER EIGHT

Shea

"Sure," I said, my pulse pounding as I accepted Holt's invitation to dance.

He took my hand and led me onto the dance floor, the curious gazes of bystanders following us. We'd be the talk of the town by tomorrow morning, thanks to the churning rumor mill.

He put a hand on my hip and I silently warned myself to be cool. I didn't come to these things often because I was usually busy planning the next day's menu and closing down the kitchen for the day. Evenings were my quiet time.

Grady and Avon had talked me into coming tonight, though, and I'd expected to just hang out with them and talk. The only men I'd danced with in a long time were Grady and Coulter. There was no possibility of sparks flying between me and my brother's best friend.

With Holt, though? There was an entire gymnastics meet happening in my stomach. I was used to having his kids as a buffer between us, the attention mostly on them.

"You okay?" he asked me as we moved in time to the music.

"Yeah, I'm good."

We were close enough that I could detect notes of cedar in his cologne. He wore a short-sleeved button-down shirt, jeans and cowboy boots, looking every inch the Beard native he was.

There was also an element of newness, though. He'd changed since leaving right after high school to play pro hockey. I felt a pull not just toward the boy I'd crushed on but the man he'd become.

"Hey, I have a favor to ask," he said.

"Sure, hit me."

The corners of his lips tugged up in a sheepish grin. "Spencer told me he wants you to teach him how to cook since his old man is so terrible at it."

I laughed. "Is that true?"

"Entirely. When my ex-wife left, I was still playing hockey, so I had to hire a full-time nanny and she cooked for the kids. But once I retired, I wanted to take care of the kids on my own. We all learned some hard lessons that first month or so."

"Ah, but you were doing your best, I'm sure."

"I turned a bunch of white clothes pink because I didn't know you shouldn't wash a brand-new red hoodie with whites," he said. "Spencer was pissed about his Science Camp shirt getting ruined."

"I'm sure he forgave you."

"I made spaghetti with undercooked noodles one night. We ended up putting the meat sauce on garlic bread and throwing out the noodles."

I felt a tug in my chest as I imagined Holt trying to learn so much about raising children, cooking and taking care of a house all at once.

"That sounds delicious," I said.

He grinned. "Not gonna lie, it was amazing. I've made just sauce and garlic bread for dinner a few times since then."

"You want me to give you cooking lessons?" I said.

"If you can spare the time. I'll pay you, of course."

"Of course I have time, and you're not paying me."

His eyes were possibly locked on my lips, and I was more than okay with it. I was warm all over, and it wasn't from the movement of dancing.

"I don't suppose you want to learn to play

hockey?" he asked with a wink. "We could trade lessons."

I laughed and arched a brow. "I'm a Grady. I learned how to play hockey before I could speak in full sentences."

"Ah. That's right. I could probably still show you a thing or two, though. I've been told I'm an okay player."

The thought of being on the ice with Holt and seeing him in his element was more than a little enticing. I'd watched his games on TV many times, and never had I even dreamed he'd offer me one-on-one lessons.

"I play in a rec league, so I'll take you up on that."

"What position?"

My mind immediately went to sex. I flushed as I fought the urge to blurt out something inappropriate.

"In hockey, dirty girl," Holt said with a grin.

Oh God. I wanted to melt into the floor. He knew what I'd been thinking. And worse, my body temperature had just risen several degrees when he called me *dirty girl*.

"Usually defense. It depends on how many players we have. Sometimes I play *O*."

O, as in offense, not orgasm, but again, my mind was like a runaway freight train of sexual thoughts.

How could it not be, with my hand on the shoulder of Holt Sellers, our bodies just inches apart?

His eyes were locked on mine, his hand more on my back than my hip now. I imagined him sliding it beneath the hem of my shirt, his fingers grazing my bare skin.

"Well, before you allow me into your kitchen," he said, "I have some good news for you."

"What's that?"

"I always wash my hands after I piss."

I furrowed my brow for a second, cringing when I realized what he was talking about.

"Spencer overheard me telling an employee that."

Holt's grin was amused. "Is that what happened? All he told me is that Shea wants people to wash their hands after they piss."

I burst into nervous laughter. "I'm so sorry. I didn't know he was there when I said that. I'd never"

He put a fingertip over my lips, stopping me. "It's okay. They've heard much worse from me."

"Oh yeah?"

He shook his head. "The kids and I were out for pizza a few months ago and I was hangry. We'd been waiting for more than an hour and I was grumbling. So the server, who's probably a teenager, comes up to the table to apologize and Marley says, 'My dad wants to know where our fucking pizza is.'"

"Oh no!" I laughed. "Marley?"

"I know, right? It's so unlike her. But she's really latched on to me since the divorce, and if she thinks somebody's doing me dirty, she's all over them."

"That's really sweet."

"She's a doll. She likes her hair braided this certain way her mom used to do it. It's called double Dutch braids. You know what that is?"

I nodded. "I do."

"Well, I've been watching YouTube videos about how to do it and she just sits there patiently and lets me try over and over."

The image of Holt trying to braid Marley's hair left a mushroom cloud in place of my ovaries. It was unbelievably sexy that he worked so hard at being a good dad.

He'd left behind fame, millions of dollars and a chance at championships and records, all to raise his children. And from what I'd seen, he had no regrets.

"Do you miss hockey?" I asked him.

"I thought I would. I'm not ashamed to say I cried many tears at the end of my career because I didn't think I was ready to retire. I played for thirteen years and I loved every minute. But I'm good. My kids need me more."

"You're a great dad."

The music had switched to a faster pace, but we

were still slow dancing, oblivious to the world around us.

"Thanks, but I haven't always been," he said. "I missed a lot of my kids' early childhood because I was so focused on hockey. Even in the offseason, which is when I did endorsement stuff and offseason training. My ex-wife..." He looked away and then back at me. "She said she cheated on me because she felt like a single mom, and I'm not excusing what she did, but...I own that I should have been a better partner and parent."

He was a unicorn, a man who was emotionally healthy enough to own his shit and not blame everyone but himself for his issues. Every man I'd ever dated had been...well, *not* a unicorn.

The music stopped and we stood together in silence for a few seconds as the singer for the band announced they were taking a break.

"Hey!" a voice boomed from nearby. "Music's over, asshole. And that's *my sister*."

Holt and I both turned to find Grady glaring at us. I rolled my eyes at him.

"Fuck off, Grady."

My brother didn't like it when men so much as looked at me, and he about jumped out of his skin if he saw someone actually touching me. To him, I was eternally his innocent, underage little sister.

"Let it go, man," Holt said to Grady. "She's not wearing a habit."

Grady's jaw dropped with disbelief. He wasn't used to people giving his shit right back to him.

Grady pointed at Holt as we left the dance floor. "If you take advantage of my sister, I'll"

"Whoa there." Avon inserted herself between Grady and Holt. "Let's go get some air, babe."

Coulter joined the two of them. "Yeah, it's definitely time for some fresh air. Let's go."

Holt and Grady's gazes were locked in an alpha male stare-off. I tried to lead Holt in the opposite direction, but he wouldn't budge.

Finally, Grady left with Avon and Coulter. I breathed a sigh of relief.

"I didn't do anything wrong," Holt said, his eyes apologetic. "I'm not backing down from him when I didn't do anything wrong."

Men. I didn't understand why they had to piss on things and pound their chests to prove their virility.

"I know," I said. "My brother isn't reasonable about some things."

He nodded. "He's always been that way."

"Always."

Holt looked from side to side. "Something smells amazing."

"I think it's potato skins. They make killer potato skins here."

"You feel like getting some food?"

I nodded. "I'm famished. And thirsty."

"Let's do it, then. I bet you don't get many meals you didn't have to cook yourself."

I laughed. "I don't eat the stuff you guys get in the dining hall. I'm lucky if I get to scarf a muffin or a turkey sandwich during the day."

"That's not cool."

I shrugged. "I love cooking for other people. That's the fun part of it for me."

"Have you always loved it?"

"As long as I can remember. I always wanted to help my mom in the kitchen."

We walked into the dining side of The Barn, where Holt found a small, open table for two.

"Tell you what," he said as we both sat down. "You teach me a few things in the kitchen, and then I'll make you a fantastic dinner."

My stomach flipped at how date-like his invitation sounded.

"I'm in," I said.

"I'll cook for you in my new kitchen. My house should be done in about a month."

"How's it coming?"

He smiled, his eyes sparkling with happiness. "I love it. You should come by and see it sometime."

"I'd like that."

I didn't know what I was doing. Because I wasn't the kind of woman who messed around with a single dad. Especially not one so fresh off of his last relationship, trying to raise his kids completely alone.

But the time I'd spent with Holt was the longest I'd gone without thinking about work in a very long time, and it felt good.

I'd go home to my little bungalow on Main Street alone later tonight. But until then, I was going to enjoy myself and let my worries catch up with me tomorrow.

CHAPTER NINE

Holt

"My man!" Grady called out as he approached me in the lobby of The Sleepy Moose.

I stood and shook his outstretched hand, unsure what he was doing here. Marley was doing a bug-catching day camp for kids staying at The Moose, and Spencer was helping Shea in the kitchen. I was using the few hours of alone time to catch up on emails at a quiet little nook on one end of the lobby.

"You're on Team Grady!" my friend said, still pumping my hand. "For the showdown! We're gonna dominate!"

"Oh." I grinned, his enthusiasm contagious. "Hey, let's do it."

"I assume you can train anytime?"

"Train?"

"Yeah, we're not taking any chances. The events are archery, ring toss, pole climb, an obstacle course and rowing."

I ran my hand over my face, where my beard was getting long and thick enough for a trim.

"Okay, and who are we doing this with?"

He put both hands on my shoulders. "We didn't get Georgette. It's in the bag."

"Okay," I said, not really understanding what he meant. "Well, I have my kids, but if I know in advance, I can drop them at my parents' house when I need to...uh, train."

"Excellent. I was thinking we could put the trophy at the hockey complex instead of the police station. That way, more people will see it."

"Sure." I scratched my head. "So we're guaranteed to win, but we're still going to train?"

"That's right. You never know. Georgette could drop out between now and showdown day. We have to be prepared."

"Sure, buddy. Whatever you need from me."

He was about to respond when he stopped to listen to a voice on his police radio.

"Damn, I have to go," he said. "I'll get a training schedule together later."

"Looking forward to it," I said, sitting back down.

He was walking toward the door when he turned around and walked back to me.

"Hey, do you want to be one of my groomsmen?"

I arched my brows, surprised. "Sure, I'd love to."

"Great. We already have six bridesmaids and six groomsmen, but it feels like you should be there, so Avon's going to ask someone else to keep the numbers even. I mean, I would have asked sooner, but I didn't know you all that well, and with working on the complex..." He shrugged. "I just have a feeling we're going to stay great friends."

"Me too, man. Thanks for asking me. I'd be honored to stand up there with you."

He looked away for a second and then back at me. "There is one thing I need from you, though."

I grinned. "You want me to throw you a bachelor party?"

"Nope, Coulter's the best man and he's got that covered. Your ass better be there. The thing I need is for you to stay away from my sister."

My jaw dropped. "Sorry, what?"

His expression was sheepish. "I saw the way you were looking at her the other night at The Barn. I fully support your rebound activities and all, but not with my sister."

I cleared my throat. "Grady, you were the one

who suggested I find a rebound thing. I never even thought about it."

"The first one after a big breakup is always the rebound. Have you been with anyone since the divorce?"

I looked from side to side, not really wanting to discuss my sex life in the lobby of The Sleepy Moose.

"No."

"Yeah, so I'm gonna need you to start envisioning Shea with a hooked nose and warts all over. Whatever you have to do. I don't want to have to beat the shit out of one of my groomsmen."

I was about to laugh when I realized he was dead serious. I took a breath in and let it out, choosing my words carefully.

"You know she's a grown woman, right?"

"She's still my little sister. And with us coaching together, the last thing we need is tension. If you break my sister's heart and I have to break your nose...tension. See what I mean?"

It amused me that he thought I'd let him break my nose. I wasn't as big as Grady, but I was no slouch, and I'd played pro hockey for more than a decade. Fighting had been part of my job.

"This is a nonissue, because, like I told you the other day, I'm not interested in getting involved with anyone."

He nodded. "If that changes, don't make a move on Shea. We good?"

This whole interaction had been confusing as hell. Grady had asked me to be a groomsman in his wedding and threatened to kick my ass in the same conversation.

"Yeah, we're good," I said.

Not because he'd scared me into submission, but because, like I'd said, it was a nonissue. I was focused on my kids, my house and the hockey complex. And now, apparently, training for the Summer Show-down so Grady could hoist a trophy.

I liked to avoid pissing matches when I could, especially with friends.

————

"I POURED everything in the bowl. The bread crumbs and the milk and...there was other stuff, but I don't remember what it was. Dad, are you listening?"

I slid my phone into my pocket after returning a text from my agent. "Yep. Bread crumbs. Milk. Meatloaf."

"And then Shea let me squish some together. It was really cold."

I ruffled his hair. "Well, you guys did a great job. That meatloaf at dinner was the best I've ever had."

"Better than Grandma's?"

"Well...yes, but don't tell her I said that."

Marley inhaled sharply from the lawn chair next to mine. "Daddy, he just ate fire! He ate it!"

We were on the large lawn of The Sleepy Moose for the evening activities, which included a juggler, a fire eater, making s'mores, live music and fireworks. Marley was staring wide-eyed at the fire eater, but Spencer was more excited about his work in the kitchen with Shea earlier.

"He's not really eating fire, Mar," I said. "Don't ever try to do that."

"He is, Daddy!" She pointed and stood up. "Look at him, he's *eating* it."

"It's like a magic trick. He's not eating fire."

"Fire would burn his mouth, Marley," Spencer said, shaking his head.

"Well, if it isn't Holt Sellers," a female voice said.

I looked up to find a dark-haired woman smiling at me. She looked familiar, but I couldn't place her. Wearing a dark miniskirt and a slinky black top, she looked like she was dressed for a night at a club rather than an evening on the lawn at The Sleepy Moose.

"I'm Tara Johnson. I was one year behind you in high school," she said.

I stood to shake her hand. "Yeah, I remember you. Good to see you again."

She brushed her long bangs away from her eyes. "I heard you moved back. Figured I'd run into you eventually."

"Yep." I gestured at Spencer. "This is my son Spencer and my daughter Marley. Guys, this is..." I looked at Tara. "Is it Miss or Mrs.?"

She laughed loudly and waved a hand. "Oh, it's Miss. I haven't found anyone who made me want to settle down...yet."

She wasn't subtle, that was for damn sure. I'd figured there would be single women in the Beard who wanted to try to land a man with an eight-figure bank account, but right in front of my kids?

"Miss Johnson," I said.

"Nice to meet you, Miss Johnson," my kids said.

"Aw." She put a hand on her chest. "Such great manners. How old are you guys?"

"I'm six," Marley said, still gazing at the fire eater.

"Nine," Spencer said.

"Oh." Tara looked at me and bit her lip. "My two favorite numbers. Especially when you put them together."

Classy. I gave her a tight grin, wishing I knew how to make her move along.

"That makes fifteen," Spencer said.

"Yes, it does, sweetie," Tara giggled and touched a fingertip to the tip of his nose.

Spencer scowled in my direction. I cleared my throat and sat back down.

"It was great seeing you, Tara. Take care."

"Shea!"

Spencer jumped out of his chair and ran across the lawn. Shea had just walked out, and he slid his hand into hers. I about fell out of my chair. My son hadn't let his mom hold his hand in years.

Spencer gazed adoringly up at Shea, and she smiled down at him. I felt a catch in my chest. He kept his emotions closer to the vest than Marley did, and he pretended to be fine with not having his mom in his life anymore.

But seeing the way he looked at Shea cut me deep. She fulfilled something in him that I'd never be able to. I loved my kids more than anything, but I couldn't nurture them the way a mother figure could.

Shea had a folded-up lawn chair under one arm, and she set it up next to Spencer's and waved at me and Marley.

"Hi guys, how are you? Hi, Tara."

"That man just ate fire, Shea," Marley said, still spellbound.

"Ouch. I hope someone gave him some water after."

Tara was clearly trying to decide whether to stay or go. She leaned down to Marley's level.

"Hey, do you want to get some ice cream?"

Marley's expression brightened and she looked at me. "Daddy, can I?"

There was a big window area open at the back of the lodge where people could buy drinks, snacks and ice cream. But there wasn't a chance in hell I was letting someone I'd just met take my kid several hundred feet away from me.

Better to be overprotective than not protective enough. Even in my small hometown.

"I'm taking them over to get some snacks in a little bit," I said to Tara.

"Okay, well...it was nice seeing you," she said, finally giving up and walking away.

I sat back in my chair, relieved she'd given up. I hadn't foreseen women using sexual innuendo in front of my kids, and I definitely didn't like it.

"Maybe we should get some ice cream for the man who ate fire," Marley said.

"That's a great idea, peanut."

We stood and I asked Shea and Spencer if they wanted anything.

"Shea loves strawberry ice cream cones," Spencer said.

Shea grinned. "That's true, but I'll go get one in a little bit."

"One strawberry cone, coming up," I said. "What about you, Spence?"

"Chocolate cone, please."

Marley and I went to get the ice cream, and she only came close to dropping her dish of vanilla with blueberry topping and Spencer's cone twice on the walk back. I'd almost made it when I noticed Shea's cone was about to drip, so I swiped that spot with my tongue.

"I gave it a little lick so it wouldn't drip on you," I said as I handed it to her.

"Thanks. It looks delicious."

"You can try mine if you want to," Spencer said as his sister handed him his cone.

"Thank you." Shea gave Marley a warm smile. "That looks so good, Marley. You have great taste."

Marley thanked her, blueberry topping already smeared around her mouth.

"What did you get, Dad?" Spencer asked.

"Chocolate peanut butter cone."

"My dad loves peanut butter," Spencer told Shea. "We should make him some peanut butter cookies."

"That's a great idea."

I met her gaze in a quick, grateful look. Spencer was crazy about her, and seeing him so happy meant more to me than my own happiness.

There had been a lot of tears and counseling sessions between Andrea leaving and now. And while I'd promised my kids we'd thrive in our new town, it was gratifying to finally see it actually happening.

CHAPTER TEN

Shea

"Shea." Avon closed her eyes and moaned with happiness as she took another bite of raspberry filling while standing in the nearly empty kitchen at The Sleepy Moose. "I would maim for that. It's definitely going to be the cake filling, but can I also have a separate bowl of it just to eat?"

I laughed, pleased by how much she liked it. "You're the bride. You can have anything you want."

"What I really want is for Grady to stop stressing about the wedding. Did I tell you he's trying to train Wayne to walk down the aisle?"

I scrunched up my face in confusion. "Your dog?"

"Our dog. He wants him to be the ring bearer, but there's no way Wayne can walk past that many people without stopping. At the first *aww*, he'll be waddling over for snuggles."

"As he should."

I loved the bulldog my brother had given his future wife when he proposed. He was lazy, sweet and a great cuddler. If I had the time, I'd get one just like him for myself.

"I think Grady should have one of the groomsmen walk Wayne down the aisle on a leash," Avon said. "He won't quit, though. He's out there in the yard every evening with a fake red carpet rolled out, trying to teach Wayne to walk down it without stopping."

I laughed at the image because Wayne didn't even walk across a room without flopping down partway for a rest.

"Maybe if someone's holding a steak at the altar?" I suggested.

"A leash would simplify everything."

"When Grady puts his mind to something..."

Avon rolled her eyes. "I know, forget about changing it. I'm hoping he won't have time for the Wayne thing anymore now that the showdown teams have been announced."

I opened a small refrigerator where we kept ingredients we needed close while cooking and took out a small saucer, passing it to Avon.

"Cannoli?" she cried. "We're having cannoli?"

"If you want to."

She took the fork I offered her and sampled a bite, moaning again. "Oh my God, yes. The cannoli is a hard yes."

"Got it," I said, making a check mark on the paper I had on a clipboard. "I'm making your two main course options this weekend at my parents' house for Sunday dinner. That way, Grady has a say about something without ruining anything."

I reached for the saucer with the cannoli Avon had taken a bite of, but she protested. "Don't throw that away, I'll finish it."

"Sure, but you also have a bunch of side dishes to taste."

"I'll save it for dessert."

I went to the walk-in cooler and picked up some small containers of side dishes I'd prepped, and when I got back to the stainless-covered kitchen island, Avon was giving me a funny look.

"What?" I asked her, taking the lid off the scalloped potatoes to warm them up.

"Holt Sellers."

My stomach flipped at the mention of his name. "What about him?"

"Don't be coy with me. We're almost sisters."

I shrugged. "There's nothing going on between us if that's what you mean."

"I saw the way you guys were looking at each other while you danced the other night. And I heard you went to a family event here with him and his kids."

I sighed softly, wanting to ask her if she'd heard what I had for breakfast this morning and what color of underwear I was wearing. The gossip mill in Sven's Beard churned steadily enough to power the entire town.

"Spencer asked me to sit with him at the event. He's been helping out in the kitchen. He's such a sweet kid."

Avon arched her brows, her arms crossed. "What does he have to do with Holt licking your ice cream cone?"

I laughed at how much that sounded like a euphemism. "Girl, it's been forever since a man licked my ice cream cone. Like years."

"Well then? Why not Holt?"

I thought about it while I busied myself warming up the scalloped potatoes and the loaded mashed potatoes I'd made earlier and left on the stove.

"I'm not trying to get to him through his kids," I said. "I genuinely like Spencer and Marley and it breaks my heart that their mom just left them."

"Of course you're not," Avon said. "I know you'd never do that. But if you like both him and his kids...then what's the problem?"

I turned to face her. "You should have seen the way Tara Johnson was all over him the other night. She was trying to get to him through Marley and it made me mad."

"Like jealous mad?"

"No, like *back the fuck away from his children* mad. Those kids have been through so much already. Their dad is the only parent they have left. And maybe they'll be ready to share him someday, but they just got here. Their house isn't even finished yet. They need time."

"I get that. But what if some other woman swoops in while you're holding back?"

Shrugging, I said, "I'm not holding back. We danced, that's it. He hasn't mentioned more because he doesn't want more."

"He was looking at you like he wanted more at The Barn."

Priscilla walked into the kitchen and I quickly changed the subject.

"So we're down to these two options for potatoes and then you need to choose two vegetables," I said.

"Grady wants cooked carrots."

I groaned. "I can roast carrots, but I wouldn't serve plain boiled carrots to anyone. Ever."

Avon laughed. "I know. He likes them boiled with loads of butter and pepper."

"He also likes boiled hot dogs and bologna sandwiches. He has the palate of a toddler."

"Let's definitely plan for broccolini, and we'll say TBD on the second veggie."

"Well, it's not one of my top choices, but I do have a great roasted carrot recipe," I said begrudgingly.

"I was actually thinking scalloped corn, maybe?"

"I love scalloped corn," Priscilla said from the other side of the room. "Sorry for interrupting. I'm just hungry. I need to go eat lunch."

I waved her over. "Come try these potatoes with us."

I prepared three plates, each with a small serving of each kind of potatoes. We all sampled them in silence.

"Damn, those are both amazing," Avon said.

"I'm really liking the loaded mashed," Priscilla said. "Especially if you're doing scalloped corn."

"I agree," I said.

"That sounds perfect to me," Avon said. "Just don't mind Grady balking over not having baked potatoes."

I scoffed. "The absolute audacity of that man to suggest I serve baked potatoes at a wedding. Why don't we have ribs, too?"

"Who's having ribs?" a deep voice said. "Am I invited?"

We all turned to see Holt grinning at us as he walked into the kitchen. He wore black shorts, a gray Mammoths T-shirt and a hat with the word "Ferda" on it.

"You like Letterkenny?" I asked, forgetting everything else.

"Hard yes," he said, grinning back.

He liked my favorite show ever. There were a lot of Letterkenny fans in northern Minnesota, but knowing Holt liked it hit differently. It told me a lot about his sense of humor. Namely, that it was awesome.

"I love that show," I said.

"Yeah, I noticed your shirt at The Barn the other night and thought you might like this hat."

We just stared at each other for a few seconds before Avon cleared her throat.

"Hi Holt," she said.

He turned to her, seemingly just realizing there were two other people in the room with us.

"Oh, hey Avon. How are you?"

"I'm good. I was just leaving, actually. Shea was

letting me taste some of her delicious options for the wedding reception dinner."

"Sounds like fun. I'm stoked about being included as a groomsman, by the way."

"Grady and I are so glad you said yes."

"Absolutely."

I glanced at my future sister-in-law, who had conveniently failed to mention Holt would be a groomsman in the wedding. We'd have to discuss that later.

"Holt, this is Priscilla," I said, gesturing to the other side of the island. "Priscilla, this is Holt Sellers, one of our guests."

"Nice to meet you," he said.

"You too."

He gave me a sheepish look. "I'm a little early. I can come back."

"No!" Avon answered before I could. "We were just leaving, weren't we, Priscilla?"

The next hour was the quiet period between finishing lunch cleanup and starting dinner prep, but Priscilla was still supposed to be polishing water spots off the cutlery. She took Avon's cue, though, grabbing a big bowl to put the cutlery in so she could polish it elsewhere.

"Bye, guys!" Avon said, swiping the cannoli on her way out.

My cheeks were warm from her complete lack of subtlety. Holt and I had planned to meet up this afternoon so I could show him a few cooking basics, but I was pretty sure we both felt like we'd been set up on a blind date after Avon's theatrics.

"So, how are the kids?" I asked as an icebreaker.

"They're great. My parents took them out to my uncle's farm for the day. They'll be milking cows and fishing in the lake."

"That sounds like a perfect summer day to me."

He set a glass jar on the island. "Thought you might like some of my mom's berry jam."

"Thank you. I'm sure I'll love it."

He gave me a tentative look. "Are you sure you have time for this? Because I can come back another time."

"This is a great time." I looked down at my apron to make sure there was no food on it. "Is there anything you want to start with? Do you know how to make scrambled eggs?"

"Yeah, but they always stick to the pan."

I smiled and headed for the walk-in cooler. "The answer is butter!" I cupped a hand around my mouth like I was telling him a secret. "In cooking, the answer is often butter."

He washed his hands and I gave him two eggs to crack into a stainless bowl. He swore several times and had to pick little eggshell bits out of the bowl, but he got the job done.

"What's the secret to not getting shells in there?" he asked.

"Practice."

He passed me two eggs. "Let's see how you do it."

I cracked each egg against the counter at the same time, then positioned them over the bowl and let the contents fall into the bowl. Holt arched his brows and grinned.

"I'm never cracking an egg in front of you again."

I smiled. "I've cracked thousands of eggs over the years. It just becomes second nature." I pass him a whisk. "Whisk until they're combined but not frothy."

While he whisked, I added in a splash of Worcestershire sauce and ground fresh salt and pepper into the bowl. When he was done whisking, I passed him a hand grater and a block of fresh cheddar.

"Grate and I'll tell you when," I said. "This is going to be about one-eighth of a cup, just enough to add some flavor."

He grated until I told him to stop. I showed him how to measure two tablespoons of butter and add them to a skillet.

"When it melts, move the skillet around to coat the whole bottom," I say.

Soon, he was pouring the eggs into the skillet and I showed him how to gently move them with a spatula.

"Okay, time to remove it from the heat," I say when they're done.

He lowered his brows with concern. "Okay, I've been overcooking scrambled eggs my whole life."

"That's okay, most people do."

Once the eggs are on a plate, I get two forks and we exchange a look.

"I have a great feeling about these," he says.

We both got a bite at the same time, and he groaned as he got a taste of the finished product.

"Those are seriously the best eggs I've ever had."

"I get our eggs and butter from the most amazing little organic farm. It's amazing how much the way food is grown and raised affects the flavor."

He just looked at me for a second, his attention unnerving.

"What?" I ask.

"Sorry." He looked away and then back at me. "I just like your enthusiasm for what you do. It's so clear you love this."

I sighed softly. "I'm here at least sixty hours a week, so I guess it's good that I love it."

His expression changes and he looks away.

"Don't miss out on life for your work. I learned that lesson the hard way."

"What do you mean?"

"My ex-wife and I are completely over, but in the aftermath of what happened with us, I went to counseling and it helped me realize what I did to contribute to the end of the relationship. I should have been more present for her and the kids, but I gave most of my time and energy to hockey."

I opened my mouth to respond, then closed it again.

"What were you going to say?" he asked.

"Something I thought better of."

He nudged me. "What?"

"There's no excuse for cheating. That's my opinion, anyway."

"Trust me, I agree. But I wouldn't have the relationship I do with my kids if my ex hadn't cheated and left." He shrugged. "I'm grateful I made the changes I did, no matter what made me do it."

"That makes sense. Spencer and Marley are lucky to have you for a dad."

He smiled. "Thank you."

"How about if I show you how to make a really good butter garlic chicken? It's usually a kid favorite when we make it here."

"Sounds amazing."

I gathered ingredients for the next dish, remembering what I'd said to Avon less than an hour ago.

No matter how attracted I was to Holt, he was still finding his footing as a single dad. I needed to keep my distance. If I stayed nothing more than a friend to him, Spencer and Marley, I'd never have to worry about things going south after a breakup.

So, as hard as it was, I kept the focus on cooking.

Mostly. I couldn't help sneaking a few glances at his arm muscles in his T-shirt.

CHAPTER ELEVEN

Holt

"Dad, can Shea show you how to make these?" Spencer asked through a mouthful of banana walnut pancakes.

"I'll ask her."

Both of my kids had devoured a stack of pancakes and several pieces of bacon, but since it was Summer Showdown day, I'd gone lighter with some toast and scrambled eggs. I was going to miss waking up and coming to the dining hall for breakfast here. Work on our house was coming along nicely, but I'd reserved our suite here for another month and I already knew we'd stay for every day of it, even if the house was ready for move-in sooner.

Melanie and Sylvia, two older guests at the inn, approached our table, both smiling at Marley.

"Okay, let's see how Dad did today!" Melanie said.

They checked the back of her hair and both gave me a thumbs-up.

"I couldn't have braided it better myself!" Sylvia said. "At least, back before I had arthritis. I couldn't braid anything these days."

Marley beamed at me. I'd decided to think of double Dutch braids like hockey. When I was younger, I drilled hockey essentials over and over until I got them. So I took the same approach—watching videos and practicing again and again. Marley played a handheld video game to make the time pass easier.

And now, here I was, a pretty damn good hair braider.

"You did good, Holt," Melanie said, cupping my cheek in her soft hand.

"Thanks."

"We heard you'll be part of the big race today," she said.

"Yes, ma'am."

"Good luck."

"Thank you."

Melanie's husband, Ron, approached our table, putting his hands on Spencer's shoulders.

"Did you save me any pancakes?" he asked.

Spencer smiled and shrugged. "They were really good."

"That's okay, son. You're a growing boy."

"And you're turning out to be a handsome one," Sylvia said.

Spencer's cheeks turned pink, but I could tell he enjoyed the compliments. The other long-term summer guests here had gotten to know us and my kids loved having a little extended family here.

"Did you hear there's a baby moose on Main Street?" Ron asked me.

"No. Just walking around?"

"That's what it was doing yesterday when we were at the bookstore. The mama and daddy moose were close by. The locals call them Floki and Helga."

Marley turned to me with wide eyes. "Can we go see the baby moose, Dad? Please?"

"We'll try. But not today. Today's the showdown."

A hostess came over to tell Melanie, Sylvia and Ron their table was ready. While the kids finished eating, I glanced around the dining hall, hoping to catch a glimpse of Shea.

It had been five days since our last cooking lesson, and I missed seeing her. The kids had been spending lots of time with my parents and I'd been at the current youth hockey complex, meeting players and their families and starting plans for the transition to the new location.

My days were full, and other than Andrea sending texts regularly asking if we could talk on the phone, I had no complaints. But no matter how many people I talked to or how much I accomplished in a day, it was always a better day when I got to talk to Shea, even if only for a little bit.

"Dad, she's in the kitchen," Spencer said.

"Hmm?"

He pushed his glasses up on his nose. "Shea. You were looking for Shea, but she's in the kitchen. She's short-staffed this week and she has to be in the kitchen a lot."

Spencer still got to see Shea often. He stopped by the kitchen just to say hi all the time. But I'd gotten a vibe from her during our cooking lessons that she wanted to keep things platonic, so I didn't want to just drop in on her.

Okay, I *did* want to drop in on her, but I didn't think she wanted me to. This situation was like high school all over again.

"I wasn't looking for her," I said.

Spencer gave me a *you're pathetic* look. "Yes, you were, Dad."

I set my napkin on my plate, ignoring him. "Are you guys ready?"

"Where are we going?" Marley asked.

"You guys are coming to warm up with me. Grandma and Grandpa will be here soon and then you'll hang out with them."

Grady had given me two of the "Team Grady" shirts our team was wearing for the kids, and they were excited about watching the competition. I hoped we won, but it was no longer a lock because Georgette, the weakest member of the fire chief's team, had sprained her arm practicing and was out. She'd been replaced with a college football player who was home for the summer working part-time delivering flowers for her shop.

When the kids and I approached my team on the lawn of the inn, Grady nodded at me, his expression serious. Deadly serious. This competition meant a lot to him.

"Dina, have you been practicing rings?" he asked one of the other team members.

"As much as I can. I'm getting better."

In our practices, she couldn't throw the rings hard enough. She couldn't get them within five feet of the wood stakes we had to hook them on. If she couldn't land three rings on stakes today, we'd be stuck at that station until the other team won.

"Why don't you go work on that?" Grady said, a line of worry between his brows. "Spencer and

Marley, your job is to collect the rings and bring them back to Dina, okay?"

My kids both nodded, thrilled to have a job to do for the showdown team. They left with Dina for the nearby ring practice area. Grady approached me, his arms folded across his chest.

"I think we've done everything we can," he said. "It's in Sven's hands now."

"The kids and I went and rubbed his beard last night," I said.

Everyone in town seemed to know relying on the ghost of Sven for luck by rubbing his statue's beard was just a superstition, but no one dared say it out loud. I liked that my kids now lived in a place with unique quirks.

"I'm going to stretch," I said.

I couldn't work out like I did when I was playing hockey full time; I had my hands full with the kids. I still did what I could, though, taking them for bike rides and hikes and getting in a run on the days they were with my parents.

Avon walked up and handed Grady a water bottle, saying hi to me on the way. She was on our team. I couldn't imagine the tension in their house if she had drawn a spot on the other team like last year. Grady was all in. This was game seven of a world championship for him.

For his sake, I hoped we pulled it off.

———

"Use your legs!" Grady bellowed at Dina a few hours later. "Grip it!"

The rest of our eight-person team had completed the pole climb, the first event in the showdown. Several hundred people were watching, yelling and cheering for either Team Grady or Team Curt.

Curt Painter, the Sven's Beard fire chief, was every bit as invested in this competition as Grady was. I understood now—this was between the two of them. A showdown between the police and fire department heads to prove who was stronger.

Dina was making her way up the pole one inch at a time, sweat dripping from her face down to the ground.

"Come on, Dina!" I called up to her, clapping. "You've got this! Just a little bit at a time. You're almost there!"

Grady was about to lose it. Curt's team had already finished this event and there were cheers coming from the archery station, meaning people were hitting targets over there.

Fortunately, everyone on our team was strong in archery. Dina climbed a couple more inches and reached for the button at the top of the pole, smacking it and lighting it up. Our team erupted into cheers.

Grady cupped his hands around his mouth and yelled up to her. "Lean all the way back in the harness and use your feet to get back down! Lean back, you're safe!"

Dina was skittish about leaning backward while fifteen feet in the air, which I understood. Poor Grady was jumping up and down as she slowly made her way down the pole.

Once on the ground, she dumped her gear and breathed a sigh of relief.

"Let's move, people!" Grady called out like a drill sergeant. "We've got ground to make up on archery! Keep your heads in the game!"

All eight of us lined up to complete the archery event at the same time. I hadn't practiced archery much over the years, but I did so much of it as a kid growing up in the Beard that it was second nature to me. All of us finished the station quickly and moved on to the ring toss.

"Go Dina!" Marley cheered from the front of the group of bystanders. "And Daddy!"

The ring toss reminded me of putting a puck in the net at close range. It took finesse. The kids and I had been practicing it on this lawn all week, and I was ready.

Dina struggled to complete the ring toss, but one of Curt's team members was having a hard time with it, too. They finished the station about a minute before our team did.

"Go, go, go!" Grady called behind him as he led us to the obstacle course.

I wondered how he and his sister could be so different. They were both level-headed and mostly easygoing, but Grady could be intense and impatient. She was one of the most patient people I'd ever known; she never lost her cool or got frustrated with my kids or her staff. The *washing your hands after you piss* thing Spence had told me about sounded like Shea letting an employee with a shitty attitude know who was boss, and that was a good thing.

We ran around stacked tires, climbed a rope wall and belly-crawled through mud to complete the obstacle course, finishing before Curt's team.

Grady led us to the final event, which was also the hardest. We had to row a double scull out into the lake, maneuver it around a buoy, and bring it back to shore, then run through the finish line.

"Let's go, people!" he yelled out as we all scrambled into the boat. "Sit your ass down and grab your oars!"

Once we pushed away from the shore, we got into a good rhythm with the rowing. Out on the water, I hardly heard the roaring crowd. The swish of the oars in the water and the view of the expansive lake were peaceful. I could hardly wait to take my own kayak out on this very lake.

My home was miles away, but it was on Lake Karlsson, too. I'd paid a lot for a massive, private lot on the water with woods behind it, but it was worth every penny.

Curt's team was in the water now, and they were closing in.

"Row!" Grady ordered. "Come on, this is it! Don't choke now!"

We'd practiced going around the buoy, just a few of us rowing for the maneuver. As soon as we'd cleared it, Grady told everyone to start rowing again.

"Home stretch!" he called out. "Give it everything you've got!"

He picked up the pace and we rowed hard. I could hear someone behind me breathing hard. Rowing was no joke; it took a lot of energy to go this fast. Curt's team was on our heels, but we made it to shore first, Grady helping people out of the boat before taking off last from the shore.

I held back for the slower members of the team so we could all cross the finish line together. When we did, Grady jumped into the air, letting out a war cry.

My kids ran up to high-five me, avoiding hugs since I was muddy and sweaty, my parents close behind. I was enjoying the moment when I saw Shea walking up, her bright smile making me forget everything for a couple of seconds.

She hugged her brother, not caring at all about the mud and sweat. I felt a tug of something in my chest, wishing she'd hugged me instead. Or even as well.

I didn't like being ignored by her. Next weekend was the combined bachelor and bachelorette party weekend for Grady and Avon, and I planned to make sure she couldn't ignore me then.

CHAPTER TWELVE

Shea

"When's the last time you took an entire weekend off work?" Avon asked me.

"I think...two years ago?"

She took my hand as we pulled up to the sprawling luxury cabin she and Grady had rented for the bachelor/bachelorette weekend.

"Please don't think about work this weekend," she said. "Don't think about anything but enjoying yourself."

"You're the one getting married, so I'm here to think about *you* enjoying yourself," I said.

"How could I not?" She grinned as she parked her Jeep Wrangler in the horseshoe driveway. "This place is a dream. Grady and I tried it out for a weekend before we booked it and it was heaven."

"It sure was thoughtful of you kids to include me and Harry," Bess said from the back seat.

"You're the matron of honor. Of course you're included," Avon said, meeting her friend's gaze in the rearview mirror.

Bess was an absolute hoot. She and Avon bickered like they were related, but really, Bess worked for Avon at the Sven's Beard Chronicle. The other bridesmaids were Avon's cousin Harper and Avon's friends Mara, Julie, Carmen and Allie. Allie had been added to balance out the wedding party after Holt was added. The other women were arriving in another car, and the men were already here, having come up a couple of hours ago.

I was nervous about Holt being here. Spencer had been spending less time in the kitchen with me and more time with his grandparents, but I still wanted to be a friend to him anytime he needed me.

After three cooking lessons, Holt hadn't asked for more. I was half-relieved and half-disappointed because I enjoyed the time alone with him. There was an unspoken tension between us, though. I was keeping him at arm's length and he knew it.

"Let's go get our drink on," Avon said with a grin.

She was right; the cabin *was* a dream. It was huge, the main living area two open stories with a sectional and two other couches. The light gray and white decor made it feel peaceful and welcoming.

The men had brought our bags with them, so all we had to do was walk in and get drinks from the stocked refrigerator. Grady had even made a big batch of margaritas for us, and I poured one each for me, Avon and Bess and the three of us walked out to the sprawling deck that overlooked a shining blue lake.

"There's my bride!" Grady called, getting up to greet Avon with a kiss.

"Thanks for the margaritas," she said.

"Thanks for marrying me in a couple weeks," he said, touching his forehead to hers and kissing her again.

The two of them were ridiculously in love. I was thrilled for my brother, but every time I saw them canoodling this way, it reminded me that I didn't have anyone who felt that way about me.

I couldn't help letting my gaze stop on Holt, who was looking at me. He was wearing a Mammoths hat and he had a bottled beer in hand. When he smiled at me, my stomach flipped nervously.

It wasn't a friendly, welcoming smile but a knowing one, like he knew why I was looking at him and was looking back for the same reason.

I forced myself to look away, paying attention

instead to the introductions Grady and Avon were making. All of the groomsmen had grown up in the Beard, so I knew them.

Bess's husband, Harry, was sitting on a porch swing, looking happy as always. Bess went over to sit with him.

"The hot tub fits sixteen people," Avon said. "So it's the perfect size."

Bess laughed and waved a hand. "Make that fourteen. Harry and I will be in bed by nine."

I exhaled hard, my stomach swirling with nervousness. Sitting in a hot tub with Holt? Other people or not, that sounded downright dangerous.

"You can hot tub anytime," Grady said. "Get in right now if you want to."

Harry started to stand up, but Bess said, "No thank you. We're too old for swimsuits."

The other women in the wedding party arrived and got drinks. One of them, Carmen, immediately made a beeline for Holt. I couldn't watch another woman flirting with him, so I went into the kitchen to work on some snacks I had packed for Grady to bring.

I'd prechopped a bunch of veggies and bagged them up. I arranged them on a huge platter and added meats, cheeses, grapes and crackers.

I heard the sliding glass doors from the deck to

the house open when I was searching the refrigerator for the dips I made.

"Hey," a deep voice said. "Let me help with that."

It was Holt, his presence making my pulse
pound.

"It's okay, I can do it. I just need to find these
dips. Maybe I should get out some more crackers.
That doesn't look like enough."

"Shea." He walked over and set his beer on the
kitchen counter.

"Hmm?" I busied myself searching for the dips.

He came closer, not stopping until he was right
next to me and my heart was beating so hard I was
sure he'd be able to see it from the outside.

"You've been avoiding me. Did I say something to
offend you?"

I gaped at him. "No, I've just been busy."

"Shea..."

"There it is!" I took the container of olive dip out
of the fridge. "Now I just need to find the dish I
packed to serve it in."

I didn't want to have this conversation with Holt.
My feelings were a tangled mess, and I didn't want
things to get even more awkward when we were
here together for an entire weekend.

"Hey there," Carmen said, grinning at Holt as she
opened the sliding glass doors and walked in. "Some

of us are getting in the hot tub. You should put on your suit and join us."

I exhaled through my nose. Not only did I have to spend this whole weekend with Holt and pretend I didn't have feelings for him, but I also had to watch Carmen Thompson blatantly trying to reel him in.

"I'd rather hang out with Shea," Holt said.

"Sure, just come out whenever," Carmen said.

I turned to face Holt. "Hey, you don't have to—"

He covered my lips with his fingertips. "I'm here because I want to be."

His touch sent a bolt of sensation to my lips, making me break out in goose bumps. My eyes were locked on his, unable to look at anything else until the sound of people coming in made me jolt.

He dropped his hand and I cleared my throat, putting olive dip into a serving dish.

"Hey, I'm putting out snacks if anyone's hungry," I said.

"Ooh, that looks amazing," Allie said, grabbing a carrot from the tray. "What can I do to help?"

"Nothing at all."

"Hey," Grady said, pointing at me from across the room. "Remember what I told you—you aren't feeding and cleaning up after us this weekend."

I put my hands up in mock surrender. "I know! You vetoed the meals I wanted to make. At least give me a few snacks, for crying out loud. And one breakfast."

"Sadly, the ingredients for your breakfast were left behind," he said, grinning. "These snacks are the only work you're doing this weekend."

I gave him a dirty look, aggravated he'd deliberately left behind the ingredients for my sausage and egg casserole and cinnamon rolls.

Everyone went to their bedrooms and bathrooms to change, leaving me alone with Holt in the kitchen.

"Looks like you're gonna have to hot tub," he said.

I looked away, unsure how to respond.

"It's hard for you to let go and unwind, isn't it?" he asked softly. "You're so used to being busy and doing things for other people that you don't take much time for yourself."

I shrugged, feeling seen and not sure I liked it.

"Even that night on the lawn, you came there for Spence. Because he invited you."

"Of course I did."

"Just try it," he said. "You're with friends here. Let go and don't do a single thing for another person. Don't wash dishes or pour drinks. Just be. And have some fun."

He didn't realize how much he was asking of me. I'd never been a partier. I went from high school to cooking classes, then culinary school. Hospitality was a natural fit for me because I loved taking care of others.

Taking care of myself, though? That wasn't even a thought. What kind of care did I need, anyway, besides showers, sleep and the occasional decent meal?

"I don't think I have much choice," I said, sighing.

A smile played on Holt's lips as he looked at me. "I'll get in the hot tub if you will."

My lips parted as I tried to come up with an answer. The truth was that I felt self-conscious about wearing a swimsuit in front of him. I never exercised, unless the twenty thousand steps a day I got at work counted. My stomach wasn't flat. I wouldn't be wearing a skimpy bikini like some of the other women in the bridal party could get away with. I'd brought a modest black one-piece suit.

But I couldn't very well sit with Harry and Bess while everyone else was in the hot tub. Grady had robbed me of my excuse—making dinner for everyone—by having our dinners catered.

"I guess I will," I said.

"Good."

He opened the refrigerator and took out the pitcher of margaritas, refilling my glass. The first one had gone down so easily that I knew I had to pace myself with this one.

Then again, though...

I took a big, reinforcing sip of the drink, steeling myself. If I had to wear a swimsuit in front of a bunch of people, one of whom was a former hockey player with a rocking body...alcohol could only help.

CHAPTER THIRTEEN

Holt

I changed into my swim trunks in record time and was already in the hot tub when Shea walked out the sliding glass doors to join us.

She had a long robe over her suit, but she still took my breath away. Her long legs stole my attention until she stopped by a chair and took off the robe, and then my gaze just wandered up and down her body.

How could everyone else be carrying on conversations, oblivious to the beautiful woman right next to us? Shea had a tentative expression; she had no idea how stunning she was.

"There's a seat right here, Shea!" I called out.

Carmen, who had moved to sit next to me as

soon as I got in the hot tub, gave me a dirty look when I asked her to scoot over.

"Nice of you to make room for *my sister*," Grady said to me from the other side of the hot tub.

He'd never give up on trying to intimidate me, but it wasn't going to work. Shea walked over and sat down in the spot between me and Carmen, inhaling sharply as she lowered herself into the hot water.

"Isn't it heavenly?" Allie said. "I haven't been in a hot tub since before I had my kids."

"Girl, you deserve a hot tub in your home," Shea said. "And a masseuse."

"I have Stan for that," Allie said with a grin. "He considers massages foreplay, so he'll rub me down from head to toe if it gets him what he wants."

"Dang, I forgot my drink," Shea said, leaning forward to stand.

"No, stay," I said, bolting up. "I'll get it. I need another one anyway."

"Get me one, too," Coulter said.

I ended up getting fresh beers for all of the groomsmen before passing Shea her margarita and climbing back into the hot tub.

She looked relaxed, ignoring Carmen as she chattered about how sore her abs were from a workout this morning. I put my arm around Shea, careful to keep it on the hot tub and not touch her.

Grady mouthed, "That's my sister," from the other side of the hot tub. I mouthed back, "I know," and looked away. He clearly thought Shea belonged in a convent. I laughed inwardly about the very real possibility of having my invitation to be a groomsman rescinded this weekend.

This would be the longest break I'd had from my kids since retiring from hockey. Knowing they'd be having fun with my parents made it easy to come here. I'd grown so used to watching my language—mostly—and always keeping an eye on them that it was hard to get used to just sitting in a hot tub with other adults, not having a care in the world.

"Hey Grady," I said. "How did you and Avon meet?"

They exchanged a look and a smile.

"She was lost and I gave her directions," he said.

She rolled her eyes. "He chewed me out and said I looked like a tourist."

Grady shrugged. "You did and you were."

"We hated each other at first," Avon said. "Every encounter ended up in an argument."

Everyone laughed and I arched a brow. "Arguing with Grady? I can't imagine."

He gave his wife-to-be a big, tipsy smile. "She

saw the light eventually. Can't keep her hands off me these days."

"Oh, is that how it is?" she asked, her eyes dancing with happiness.

I'd never had what they did. I thought I did with Andrea. We adored each other, but once we were married, everything changed. She became demanding and nothing was ever good enough.

"Seriously, guys," Grady said. "I know it's tough to take a weekend away, especially with kids and jobs and all, and it means a lot to us that you're all here to celebrate. I still can't believe Avon is going to be my wife. She's more than a dream come true for me because I never even dared to dream of someone like her."

Avon cupped his cheeks in her hands and kissed him. "What he said."

"To Grady and Avon!" Seth, another groomsman, held his beer in the air and we all toasted.

I hadn't drunk so much in a long time. I was already light-headed. Part of me wanted to slow down so I could keep my wits because losing control around Shea could be dangerous.

A bigger part of me was already past that point, though. This weekend was a chance to let go and just have fun, and I wouldn't have another chance to do that anytime soon.

A COUPLE OF HOURS LATER, I'd ditched the idea of not touching Shea. We were back in the hot tub, my arm around her. Everyone else was inside because the caterers had just brought dinner.

"Never have I ever eaten a Hershey's Kiss," I said, continuing a game we'd started when everyone else left to eat.

"What?" She laughed and shook her head. "Everyone's eaten those."

"There's all the unwrapping and then just that tiny little bite of chocolate. I'd rather just have a candy bar."

"What's your favorite candy bar?"

"Butterfinger. I'm old school. How about you?"

She thought about it. "I like white chocolate. Especially those little balls with the soft centers."

I grinned, buzzed from all the alcohol. "It's unfortunate that you like little balls. I've got big ones."

She laughed hard at my joke, her amusement making me feel like I'd accomplished something great.

"I believe in equality for all balls," she said. "No ball shaming here."

"I can't believe mine even fit in this hot tub," I quipped. "They're enormous."

She was still smiling, her eyes fixed on mine, but the mood slowly turned serious. We were sitting so close I could see the flecks of dark brown in her amber-colored eyes.

"Never have I ever wanted to kiss someone so much," I said softly.

Her lips parted slightly. "Me?"

"Of course you. You're incredible."

She tilted her head slightly in silent invitation, and I went for it. Her lips were soft and sweet, stirring something inside me that had been dormant for a long time.

Our mouths moved together in perfect unison, her closeness making me want more. She tasted like lime juice with a hint of salt. The only thing keeping me from pulling her onto my lap was the knowledge that there were people in the house who would eventually be coming back out here.

I cupped her cheek in my hand, enjoying every second of my mouth on hers until she pulled away, breathless.

"No one's ever kissed me like that," she said softly.

"You deserve to be kissed like that several times a day."

I felt the warmth of her exhale on my lips. "I don't want to ruin my friendship with you and your kids."

Disappointment rocketed through me. "You mean you don't think of me as more than a friend? Because I never would have kissed"

"No. I think of you as more. But if I acted on it, I'd feel like Tara Johnson."

I lowered my brows. "Who?"

"The woman who came up to you that night when we were sitting on the lawn at The Moose. She just wanted to sink her claws into a hockey player, and she didn't care whether or not it was good for your kids."

I nodded. "You're no Tara Johnson, but I know what you mean. My kids have been through a lot."

She put a hand on my knee beneath the water. "You're a great dad, you know. It's one of the things I find so...you know."

I grinned. "No, what? Tell me."

She looked away, unable to hold my gaze as she said it. "Sexy. About you."

Longing hit me hard. It wasn't just arousal but a deep desire for Shea, and only Shea.

"You think I'm sexy?"

"Of course, Holt. Look at you."

I cupped her cheek in my hand again, loving the way her nostrils flared just slightly.

"Look at *you*. You're so beautiful. Every time you smile, I want to take you in my arms and kiss you."

"Really?"

Her tone made it clear she had no idea how stunning she was. I couldn't take her to my bedroom in this cabin and do all the things I really wanted to do with her, but I could make sure she knew how much I wanted to.

"You drive me crazy in that swimsuit," I said.

She furrowed her brow in disbelief. "This is a ten-year-old grannie suit. Most of the other women here have tiny little bikinis on."

"Didn't notice," I said, meaning it. "You're more beautiful, smart and sweet than any of them anyway."

She scoffed. "I think you've got your beer goggles on."

"I felt this way before today," I assured her. "Even when I'm stone-cold sober, I think you're spectacular."

She smiled. "Thank you. I spend so much time in the kitchen focused on food and service that I tend to forget I'm...you know, a woman. And I think you're spectacular, too."

I sighed softly, not wanting to ruin the moment

by bringing up my ex, but needing Shea to understand where I was coming from.

"My ex-wife got pregnant with another man's kid while we were still married," I said.

"God, Holt, I'm so sorry."

"No, it's not...I'm not telling you because of me." I took a deep breath. "She wanted to take my kids to California with her because that's where her new husband lives, but I fought her in court and won."

"I had no idea."

I nodded, remembering the day I won the most important thing I'd ever be competing for, which had nothing to do with hockey.

"They went from seeing their mom every day of their lives to never seeing her," I said. "Marley's counselor told me they went through a grieving process similar to what they'd experience if she died."

She shook her head. "I don't even know what to say. I don't have kids, but if I did, I can't imagine leaving them like that."

"I need my kids to know I'm never leaving them," I said. "And it's one thing to tell them that, but..."

Shea nodded emphatically just as the sliding glass doors opened.

Shit. Worst timing ever. Coulter stepped out onto the deck.

"Can we finish this conversation later?" I asked Shea softly.

"Yes, but I know what you're getting at. You dating a woman could make your kids worry that you'll do the same thing their mom did. And I totally get that. I don't want to be part of making them feel insecure in any way."

I rubbed her bare shoulder with my thumb, my arm still around her. "If I could, though...I mean, if I were in a position to just think about myself and be with someone, it would be you."

"You two lovebirds gonna go eat dinner?" Coulter asked.

Lovebirds. I liked the sound of that, even though it was impossible.

Others were streaming out the sliding glass doors now, and I looked at Shea. "I could eat. You hungry?"

"Starving. And it would be nice to de-raisin."

I stood up and then offered her a hand. We were both drying off when Grady came over and clapped a hand on my shoulder *much harder than necessary.*

"How's my sister?" he asked me, his words slightly slurred.

"You should ask her."

"I'm great, big brother. How was dinner?"

"Outstanding. Ribs, baked potatoes and cooked carrots."

Clearly, Grady had chosen the menu; those were some of his favorite foods.

"Let's have a shot!" he cried, raising the bottle of whiskey in his free hand.

It was the first of many shots. I ended the night stumbling to my bed, knowing I would have preferred it if Shea had come with me, but too drunk to think about it for long before I passed out asleep.

CHAPTER FOURTEEN

Shea

Reality packed a massive punch when I returned to work Monday morning after a carefree weekend at the bachelor/bachelorette party. Eight youth baseball teams and their parents had stayed at The Moose for a tournament, and Nina had done her best to handle it, not texting me until very early this morning.

I wasn't surprised to see Caden in the kitchen when I walked in at five thirty a.m., but I was aggravated. I knew him well enough to know he was waiting to unleash a full weekend's worth of stored-up complaints.

"How was your weekend?" he asked, an edge in his tone.

"Fine. Nina told me she hit some speed bumps

over the weekend."

I was trying to tell him to leave me alone so I could work on breakfast prep. I'd given Nina today and tomorrow off to make up for her long weekend covering for me, so I had extra work to do.

"'Speed bumps' is putting it generously," Caden said. "We ran out of bacon on the breakfast buffet Saturday morning for more than thirty minutes. And people told me the scones were inedible on Sunday morning. Cold potatoes and gravy at dinner Saturday. Someone put the whipped butter out on the buffet Saturday morning. That's only for dinner rolls! Little boys were slathering it on their pancakes and we had to serve regular butter with dinner because, surprise, we ran out of whipped butter."

I sighed heavily, hanging up my bag and walking over to the sink to wash my hands.

"Baseball tournaments are a nightmare. I'm not sure I would have done any better than Nina. And Caden, she's my number one. I *need* Nina. If you drive her out of here"

My boss's chin nearly hit the floor. I used the few moments of sudden silence to grab an apron from a hook and tie it behind my back.

"This isn't about who anyone likes or dislikes, Shea," he said. "Last weekend, the kitchen had so many unforced errors that the level of service was far below our standards. I had to comp so many meals that it affected our bottom line."

I shook my head, irritated. "Over what? Running out of bacon? Regular butter instead of whipped? Caden, we always struggle to keep up with the breakfast buffet when we have eight baseball teams here. I hate that buffet. And you don't have to comp an entire family's meals just because we couldn't keep up with a hundred boys' appetites at once." I went over to the walk-in cooler to get ingredients, stacking them in my arms and continuing what I was saying as soon as I came back out. "Anytime someone complains, you start falling all over yourself comping things. That's on you, not Nina. She did a damn good job on a weekend with a baseball tournament while we're understaffed."

I set out my ingredients. One of my morning cooks, Ray, nodded at us as he walked in to start baking biscuits.

Caden lowered his voice but didn't let up. "You deserve the occasional weekend off, Shea, but you have to leave someone competent in your place if you choose to be gone."

"Nina is more than competent," I fired back. "And I could tell from the text she sent me this morning that you stressed her out even worse than any of the issues she was having. We are understaffed, and this job isn't easy even when we're fully staffed."

Caden put his arms out in a gesture of frustration. "So hire people, Shea. I've given you the green light."

"I can't find anyone I want to hire! Last time I advertised, the only applicant was Jan Forbes, but with her criminal record, I'm not comfortable hiring her."

"You wanted to be a department head," Caden said, crossing his arms and ignoring my very real staffing issue. "You get paid more than anyone else in this kitchen because the buck stops with you."

"I shouldn't have to be here seven days a week. And if things were so awful, why didn't you call me? You call me when the slightest thing goes wrong."

I hadn't thought about work once the entire weekend, thanks to alcohol and being with Holt. But now that I was thinking about it, Saturday had been my first day off work without a single call, and Sunday had been my second.

"Oh, I called. I was about to call the police because I was so worried when you weren't picking up or calling back, and Nina told me that your brother blocked incoming calls to your phone for the weekend."

"What?" Now, it was my jaw on the floor.

Priscilla walked in and gave me a little wave. Caden sighed dramatically and shook his head.

"We need to finish this conversation after breakfast."

"I go straight from breakfast into lunch prep," I said. "I'll have time around two this afternoon."

"Fine," he said. "Find me whenever you can fit me in."

He left the kitchen in a huff and Priscilla walked over to me.

"You okay?"

"Yeah, other than the alarm clock going off offensively early this morning. How about you?"

"No complaints. Lenny caught an eight-pound bass on his fishing trip. Can you believe that?"

"Wow, that's great. I want to see pictures later."

She tied an apron around her waist. "Of course. How was the bachelorette party?"

"It was fun. But I'm going to have to beat my brother up for messing with my phone, and he's a lot bigger than he was the last time I beat him up. He was around seven then."

She chuckled. "He just wanted you to get a real weekend away. He told Nina to call him if there was a true emergency."

I gave her a mock angry look. "Grr. You knew about it, too?"

"Course I did. And if Caden says anything about Nina, I was here Saturday until one and that girl worked her ass off. We were going through bacon like you wouldn't believe and we didn't have enough stove space to keep up, so Nina had us cooking it on the stove and in the oven. People would run up to the buffet servers and clear the bacon out of the containers before they could even get it to the buffet."

"I hate that buffet."

"Girl, same." She gathered a few kitchen tools. "You want me to prep some sausage gravy and get it in the warmer?"

"That would be great, thanks."

She turned and pointed a whisk at me as she walked away. "Don't let Caden guilt you for taking a weekend off. You deserve a lot more time off than you get. He has no life outside of this place."

Lenny switched on the local AM radio station, which we always listened to when we were doing breakfast prep.

"...a beautiful, sunny Monday here in the Beard," Bert Stanton, one of the morning hosts, said. "We'll have Chief Painter here soon with some fire prevention tips and then we'll have a chat with Mick VanDyke, the winner of the weekend fishing tournament."

"You know what, Bert? I heard he caught an eleven-pounder," said Jeannie White, the other host.

"He was a whopper, for sure. I was there to see it. But before we talk to him and the chief, let's have a word from one of our sponsors, Mort's Bait Shop. They're master baiters."

I'd made the cherry pastries I was preparing so many times that I didn't even have to think about it. I knew every measurement and direction by heart, so my mind wandered as I scooped and stirred.

The weekend was amazing. I left work at two on Friday for the two-hour drive to the cabin with Avon and Bess, and not getting a single phone call had made it seem more like a vacation than just a weekend.

Priscilla's comment about Caden not having a life was still at the front of my mind. Usually, I didn't have much of a life outside of The Sleepy Moose, either. It was nearly impossible to. Being chef here required overseeing the menu and food prep seven days a week. No one else who worked here had been to culinary school.

Spending time with Holt at the cabin had made me feel like more than just a chef. When he looked at me and said he thought I was beautiful, I felt like a woman. He smoothed out the rough edges in my self-esteem and made me wonder what it would be like to have a life outside of this place all the time.

It couldn't be with him. My instinct to resist my attraction to him had been right. Now that he'd opened up to me about what his ex had put him and his kids through, I was even more convinced that it was too soon for him to date.

I'd always thought people saying everything was right about another person except the timing was bullshit, but I understood now. Truly caring about Holt, Spencer and Marley meant putting my selfish attraction to Holt aside to allow them more time to heal.

I smiled as I whisked baking powder into my flower, remembering the moment in the hot tub when he told me how much he liked me. Just knowing that had filled up something inside me that had been empty for a very long time.

I was desirable. My feelings for Holt had been an unexpected gift that showed me how much I was missing out on. If I could find that kind of connection with him, maybe I could find it with someone else, too.

Maybe I could even have kids of my own. Being around Spencer and Marley had reminded me how much I loved kids. Spending an hour in the work kitchen baking cookies with them filled me up more than preparing time-intensive fine cuisine did.

I was determined not to turn into Caden. He was in his midforties and often slept on the couch in his office because he had no one to go home to.

My kiss with Holt had awoken my desire, not just for him but for something more for myself.

CHAPTER FIFTEEN

Holt

"Dad, you can go now," Spencer said.

I chuckled as I set a big bag of giant marshmallows on my parents' kitchen table.

"Am I cramping your style, bud?" I asked my son.

"No, it's just...the campout is starting. Grandpa has the tents all set up and the other kids are on their way."

"And Grandma has some cookies fresh out of the oven!"

My mom presented a platter of monster cookies, my kids taking one in each hand. I grabbed one, too, saying, "Thanks, Mom."

"Thanks, Grandma," my kids echoed.

"I see a kid!" Spencer cried. "Bye Dad!"

He and Marley ran out the back door of my

parents' house to their fenced-in backyard, where a few neighbor kids had just walked through the gate with sleeping bags in hand.

My parents had planned a "campout" for Spencer, Marley and the neighbor kids they liked to play with when they visited. Dad had set up three tents and built a bonfire for later.

"They didn't get to sleep until after eleven last night because they were so excited about this," I said.

"We're excited, too," Mom said. "We missed out on doing things like this when they were younger."

"You might be less excited when you have kids running in and out of the house at two a.m."

She waved a hand. "It's fine. I'm making pancakes, sausage and eggs around nine in the morning if you want to come by for breakfast."

"Yeah, I might." I looked at my phone to see if Grady had texted me back about our plans tonight.

"You better not be working this afternoon," she scolded. "It's Svensday."

On Wednesdays in Sven's Beard, most everyone knocked off work late morning, and it was considered unacceptable to be working after noon unless you worked at the hospital or some other essential job.

"I'm just going to check out the progress on my house and the arena," I said.

"The arena is work! You need to go fishing or kayaking this afternoon. Svensdays are for feeding your soul."

No matter how old I got, my mom would never stop thinking she knew better than me. Since moving back, I'd started to learn that arguing was futile. Placating her made things a lot easier.

"That sounds nice," I said.

The timer on her oven sounded and she put on oven-safe gloves. "Take some cookies with you. Do you want me to make you a sandwich?"

"No, I'm good, Mom. Thanks for doing this campout for the kids."

"It's our pleasure."

She pulled out another sheet of cookies and gave me a stern look as I snagged another cookie from the platter.

"Don't embarrass your father and me by working on Svensdays, Holt. We care about the traditions in our town."

I gave her a wry smile. "I'll try not to be an embarrassment."

"We're thrilled for your success, but this is a town of proud people who would do anything for their neighbors, and they expect our town to be respected."

I'd just seen the house and arena yesterday, so

they hadn't changed much. My parents had done a lot for me, and my mom wasn't asking for much, really. An afternoon to myself to relax while they took care of my kids? I could handle that.

"Does Dad's friend Pete still own that property on the lake outside town?" I asked.

"He does. He tells us all the time to come out anytime."

I'd spent many happy weekend afternoons on that property, hiking and fishing with my dad. It was something I looked forward to doing with my own kids now that we lived here.

"I think I'll head over there," I said. "Tell Dad I'm borrowing a pole from the garage."

"I will. And wear bug spray, or the mosquitoes will make a meal out of you."

———

BY THAT EVENING, my hamstrings were feeling the effects of my five-mile hike in the woods. I'd showered and shaved before heading out to The Hideout, a popular local bar, to meet up with Grady.

He was at a table with a few other people, and I paused for a second when I saw Shea. She'd been on my mind constantly since the weekend, but I hadn't seen her at The Moose.

How could I casually say hi to the woman I burned for? My beer buzz had made me share more of myself with her at the cabin than I normally would have, but I wasn't sorry.

"You should quit," Avon said to Shea as I approached the table. "No matter who your boss is, that place has always taken advantage of you."

"I second that motion," Grady said, clinking his beer bottle against his fiancée's.

"Hey," he said, noticing me. "Saved you a seat."

It was right next to him, on the opposite side of the table from Shea, which I knew was no accident.

"Hey," I said, meeting Shea's eyes. "Having trouble at work?"

Her shoulders slumped as she sighed. "Still dealing with the fallout from taking the weekend off."

I furrowed my brow, confused. "Are your days off usually during the week?"

"What are these *days off* you speak of?" She smiled weakly.

"They don't let her take days off," Grady said. "Can you believe that shit?"

"Not at all?"

A protective instinct surged inside of me. If someone was taking advantage of Shea in any way, I wouldn't stand for it.

"I had Mondays and Thursdays off when I started there. But then I became the chef, and I lost my most experienced cook because he wanted the chef's job. I know I sound self-important, but it's really hard to take time off when you're in charge of the menu for every meal, seven days a week. If an order from a supplier comes in and something was substituted, I have to come up with a fix for whatever we needed that ingredient for." She waved her hand. "I won't bore you guys with all the details, but this is partly on me. I wanted everything to be just right, so I chose to come in even on my days off to make sure things were running smoothly, and then I'd end up staying, and it turned into never taking a day off."

Grady shook his head. "You should still be able to when you want to, sis. Without Caden calling you every hour to bitch about the things he could figure out himself."

Shea glared at her brother. "Thanks for screwing with my phone, by the way. That upped the tension between me and Caden by a lot."

I looked at Grady. "What did you do?"

"I blocked incoming calls from her phone over the weekend," he said, shrugging. "Because I know Caden. He has no one in his life and he somehow feels threatened when Shea isn't rotting at the inn with him, so he calls her. Christmas morning, who cares? I'll call Shea to ask if there are blueberries in the kitchen. Her birthday? Not important, I'll call her about someone saying their steak wasn't served hot."

Shea looked defeated. Since she was already stressed about work, the piling on probably wasn't helping anything.

"So I heard there's a toast of some sort by city hall tonight," I said, changing the subject.

"You haven't done the Svensday toast yet?" Avon asked.

"I spent most of my time with a six-year-old and a nine-year-old," I said, grinning. "They like to get ice cream and feed the ducks in the evening."

"Well, you haven't missed much," she said.

"Blasphemy!" Grady gave her a mock stern look. "Toasting Sven brings good luck."

"And considering you're about to marry *him*," Shea said, pointing the neck of her beer bottle at Grady, "I'd say you need all the luck you can get."

"Guess we can cancel the wedding DJ and have this comedian provide our entertainment instead."

"Oh, please." Shea put her palms together in front of her in a prayer position. "I beg you. I'll come prepared with so many photos and stories about you."

Grady scoffed. "Nothin' to tell, I came out kicking ass."

"I need to grab a drink for the toast. Who needs one?" I asked.

"I'll take a water," Shea said.

"Pussy," Grady coughed into his hand.

"I'm not exaggerating when I tell you I'm still hungover," Shea said. "I don't think I've ever had that much alcohol in one weekend."

"Water for me, too," Avon said.

Shea stared at her brother. "Just waiting for you to try calling her a pussy," she said.

Grady pressed his lips together, then said, "I'll get that water for you, my love."

Drinks in hand, we all walked out of The Hideout, Grady and Avon walking hand in hand and Shea and I trailing behind them.

"Are the kids with your parents?" she asked.

"Yeah, my parents are having a campout in their backyard for them. Roasted hot dogs, s'mores, ghost stories...I think my parents might be more excited about it than the kids."

She smiled. "That sounds like fun."

"Sorry about your work stress," I said.

She shrugged. "It's just the nature of the job."

"They're very lucky to have you. They should be bending over backward to keep you happy."

"Holt, finally!"

The hair on the back of my neck stood up at the sound of the voice that called my name. It was like hearing a ghost talking to me.

I stopped walking, shocked to see Andrea walking toward me. Her hair was darker and she wasn't pregnant anymore. I just stood there, too shocked to form words.

"Hey," she said softly, smiling as she stopped a couple of feet from me. "It's so good to see you."

"What the hell are you doing here?"

My ex-wife. In Sven's Beard. I'd never imagined her and this place coexisting this way, and it was unnerving.

"You won't take my calls, and I just...we need to talk."

I looked at Shea, whose expression told me she wanted to be anywhere but here. Of all the shitty luck, Andrea had to show up when I was with Shea.

"Shea, this is my ex-wife," I said tightly. "Andrea, this is Shea Grady."

"Nice to meet you," Andrea said, giving Shea a little wave.

"I'm going to catch up with Grady and Avon," Shea said. "I'll see you later."

I hesitated, wanting to tell her not to go, but she practically ran away. I shook my head, feeling like a fucking idiot for thinking Andrea had already done all the damage she could do to my life.

"You have no right to be here," I said.

"I wanted to see you," she said in a pleading tone, reaching for my hand. "And the kids. I miss you guys."

I stepped back. "You get to see the kids in August. It was arranged by my attorney."

"Holt." She tucked the hair behind her ear, trying to look vulnerable. "Can we go somewhere and talk?"

"No. All communication needs to come through my attorney."

She flinched, looking hurt. "I had to take three planes to get here. I've been traveling all day. And then I had to find you. Please."

All I wanted was to catch up with Shea, but in the back of my mind, I worried that Andrea would go to my parents' house and try to take the kids.

"What more could there be to talk about?" I demanded. "We signed the paperwork almost a year ago. Don't you have a baby to take care of in California?"

"I left her with a friend. Listen, I made a huge mistake. I've known it for a while. All I want is a chance."

I cut her off. "No. We're way past over and you

gave up your parental rights to go to California. That's it. There's nothing more to say."

She blinked and tears spilled onto her cheeks. "Please, I miss my family."

This was the same woman who had fucked her boyfriend in our bed while our children slept upstairs. I had no patience for her.

"Don't come here uninvited again," I said.

"I want to see my kids! They're my kids, too, and I want them back!"

I was already walking away. I'd moved on from fighting with Andrea, and I was never going back to it.

CHAPTER SIXTEEN

Shea

My flowerbeds had been weeded. I smiled as I pulled into my driveway and saw how neat my mom had made my yard look. No matter how many times I told her she didn't have to do it, she was always coming over to take care of little things for me since I spent so much time at work.

It was rare for me to actually see my yard in daylight because I so often got home after dark. Today had been particularly rough because a refrigerated supply truck had broken down on the way to The Sleepy Moose, spoiling everything inside.

I'd had to create new menus for the next couple of days and scramble to source ingredients. I was looking forward to showering and going straight to bed.

But as soon as I opened my back door and walked inside, the savory smell of slow-cooked beef made my stomach rumble. Mom had put a roast and veggies in my slow cooker. Tears pricked my eyes as I looked through the glass lid at the food inside.

It was hard for me to eat at work, and when I did, it was usually just a few bites or a quick sandwich eaten on the go. Never while sitting down. Getting to enjoy this meal in my own home, with no one talking to me or asking for anything, was exactly what I needed.

I texted my mom to thank her and had just dished up a steaming bowl of beef stew when there was an insistent knock at my door.

I smiled wearily to myself as I imagined Caden standing there, asking why I had dared to leave work.

When I opened the door, though, I saw Hilary Newton, who worked for Georgette's Flowers. She was holding a massive vase of red roses.

"I would have delivered this to The Moose, but the instructions specifically said to bring it here," she said flatly. "I was about to set up a tent in your front yard and wait for you to get here."

Flowers? I had never in my life gotten flowers. My heart raced as I imagined Holt writing out a note of apology over his ex-wife showing up last night. Not necessary at all, but incredibly sweet.

"Let me grab my purse," I said.

"No, I was tipped with the order," Hilary said, passing me the vase. "Have a good night."

"Thanks."

I closed the door and carried the vase to my kitchen table, setting it down. There had to be two dozen red roses inside, each one surrounded by greenery. I leaned in to smell the perfume of one of the buds.

Thoughts of the weekend with Holt snuck in even when I was crazy busy at work. It seemed like a far-off dream now, but seeing him last night had brought it back to the front of my mind. He was everything I ever hoped to find in a man and more: strong, kind, smart and funny.

Maybe we could figure this out, bad timing or not. I opened the card, my smile sliding away as I read the words.

Shea,

Please reconsider my offer of employment. I'll pay whatever you ask. Let's discuss it at your earliest convenience.

Keller

The flowers were from Keller Strauss? My heart sank as I read the message again.

This was about Keller wanting to make me his personal chef, nothing more. He'd written his phone number at the bottom of the card.

I needed to just get a bunch of cats and accept my spinsterhood. Cats would never let me down.

As I ate my stew and browsed Facebook photos of friends who did things other than work, I considered Keller's message. He'd pay whatever I asked?

Keller was a billionaire. He could easily pay me double or triple what I made at The Moose. I didn't want to take advantage, but maybe this was an opportunity for me. I'd get to travel with him and see new places, all while saving up a lot of money for my future.

I'd never considered a future as anything but the chef at The Sleepy Moose. I loved my work and I loved the people who worked with me, but life was passing me by. I was in my thirties now and had nothing to show for it but a home my mom had to help me take care of because of my work schedule.

Maybe this was a sign. A neon sign from the universe telling me to take a chance. Try something new. Working long hours almost every day and pining for a man who wasn't ready for a relationship wasn't working, so I had to at least meet with Keller and consider this job offer.

"YOU LOOK LOVELY," Keller said, standing up from his seat at a table for two at 3Bs as I approached him the next day.

"Thanks," I said, taking off my baseball cap and shaking out my hair.

It was a beautiful summer day in the Beard, the temperature in the midseventies. Since I was only working on kitchen prep and paperwork today, I'd dressed in my favorite worn jean overalls, a tank top and Birkenstock sandals.

Keller, on the other hand, wore a crisp pale-blue dress shirt and dark dress pants, his black dress shoes shining. He was in his early forties and starting to go gray at the temples, but it suited him.

"Hey, Shea," a server named Katie said, "what can I get you?"

"My usual iced chai, please."

"You got it. And for you, Mr. Strauss?"

He smiled at her. "Call me Keller. I'll take a black coffee, please."

"You got it."

The locals called Beard Books and Brews 3Bs, and it was my favorite place to go if I could get away from work for an hour during the day, which didn't happen much. The bookshop, with a coffee and snack bar, had eclectic furniture and lots of plants. Greenery trailed down from shelves and lined every window. And it had the best smell in the world—coffee mixed with books.

"Thanks for meeting up with me," Keller said.

"Thanks for the flowers. You didn't have to do that."

He smiled. "I was hoping to get your attention."

"Well, I suppose it worked because here I am." I glanced at the clock on the wall. "I don't mean to rush things, but I have to be back at work in forty minutes."

"Oh, sure." He tapped his fingertips on the table. "Well, let's get to it, then."

Katie delivered our drinks and Keller took a black folder from his messenger bag. It had a gold foiled "Strauss Enterprises, Inc." logo stamped on the front.

"That has information you can look over later about the benefits I offer. Healthcare, dental, retirement and all. I know you've turned me down several times, but I hear you're overworked at your present job, so I hoped we could work something out where you work for me with clearly defined time off."

"Time off has been hard to come by," I admit.

"Let's say you came to New York with me for a couple of weeks. I realize that for you, that's a twenty-four-seven commitment. You could have the following week off."

I arched my brows with surprise. An entire week off? It sounded too good to be true.

"You've got all the negotiating power here, Shea," he said. "There are many chefs I could hire, but the only one I want is you. So tell me what it's going to take."

I knew exactly how Keller liked his filet mignon cooked, and he raved about my eggs benedict, but I'd never realized food meant this much to him.

"How many people would I be cooking for?"

"Most of the time, just me and my two assistants. Sometimes I entertain, though, especially when I'm in New York. I'd say usually, those nights would be around twelve people, but as many as fifty at times. And, of course, you could always hire as much help as you need."

The thought of not being responsible for three meals a day, seven days a week, for hundreds of people was appealing. What had started as a challenge had worn me out over the years I'd been doing it.

"Shea!"

I turned to see Spencer running toward me. When he got to me, I had just enough time to open my arms for his hug.

"Hey, Spence, how are you?"

"Good. Where have you been? I haven't seen you."

My heart rate kicked up as I saw Holt and Marley approaching behind Spencer. Questions swirled in my head, but of course, this wasn't the time.

"I've been working, but you know you can stop by the kitchen anytime," I told Spencer.

"Shea, I caught a fish!" Marley said. "It was wiggly."

Holt met my gaze, putting a hand on Spencer's shoulder.

"Guys, we're interrupting."

"Not at all," Keller said. "What brings the Sellers family to 3Bs today?"

"Story time," Holt said.

A handful of children were gathered on a big rug in the book section of the store.

"And cookies." Marley looked up at her dad. "You said we could get cookies."

"Let's go pick them out," Holt said, giving me a long glance that made my heart squeeze. "See you guys later."

Once they were out of earshot, Keller cleared his throat, his expression turning serious.

"I hope I'm not out of line for asking, but are you and Holt seeing each other?"

Were my feelings that obvious? I forced myself to maintain a neutral expression as I answered.

"No. He and his kids are staying at The Moose, so I've gotten to know them, but we're not involved."

"I have to be honest with you, Shea. I heard you and Holt were at The Hideout with Grady and Avon recently and that's why I extended my offer to you."

I furrowed my brow, confused. "What does that have to do with a job offer?"

I'd never seen Keller look flustered until this moment. He met my eyes across the table.

"Part of the reason I've tried so hard to get you to come work for me is because I'm interested in you. I very much hope that spending more time together could lead to...a relationship for us."

I was the deer and he was the oncoming head-lights. It took me a few seconds to gather myself and respond.

"Keller, I had no idea."

He nodded. "You're everything I've ever wanted in a partner. Please think about my offer. Name a price and I'll have my attorney draw up a contract. I'd make you happy, Shea. Whether it's strictly a job, or more."

I got up from my seat, eager to get out of there and process this news alone. It was the most surreal conversation I'd ever had.

"Thank you so much," I said, smiling. "I'll be in touch."

I couldn't get out of 3Bs fast enough. When I was safely behind the wheel of my car driving back to work, I laughed until my stomach hurt.

What the hell was happening? My life had quickly gone from boring to overwhelming. I had no idea what I was doing anymore, personally or professionally.

I pulled up to a stop sign and checked my phone, finding a text from Nina.

Nina: Bad news. Lenny called in with the flu, and I really hate to tell you this, but I'm not feeling well myself.

Awesome. We worked so closely in the kitchen that the flu usually hit most, if not all, of us. The only upside was that I'd be so slammed at work for the next few days that I wouldn't have time to think about anything else.

CHAPTER SEVENTEEN

Holt

Shea pushed open the kitchen door and stepped out, a splatter of what looked like gravy on the front of her apron.

"Holt, hey..." She smiled and wiped a towel over the stain. "When Nina said someone was here to see me, I assumed it was Spencer."

"He and Marley are at youth bowling night with my parents."

"Ah, I remember youth bowling. I always loved it."

I'd spent the afternoon working up the courage to come find her. Though she'd never admit it, I knew she was avoiding me. Before Andrea showed up unannounced, Shea would usually come out of the kitchen at least once during every meal to say hello to guests and ask how their food was. Since that night, I hadn't seen her come out at all.

"Can you get away later so we can go somewhere and talk?" I asked.

"Um..."

"Please, Shea."

She nodded. "Okay, sure. Give me like forty-five minutes."

"Have you eaten?"

"No, but"

"We'll go get tacos from Taco Train."

"Okay. Should I meet you there?"

What I really wanted was for her to meet me in my room so I could kiss her again, but this time, I wouldn't stop. It was agonizing trying to be a dad every minute of the day, pretending I didn't have other wants and needs.

And Shea was in between the two. I wanted her so badly it was becoming more like a need. I lay in bed at night, aching to be back in the hot tub with her, feeling her warm skin against mine.

"Meet me in the lobby. I'll drive," I said.

I was waiting in the lobby when she walked in forty-five minutes later, her apron gone and her hair taken down from the bun it had been in. She wore black pants and a white T-shirt, but as usual, my attention was drawn to her smile.

"I probably smell like beef gravy," she said, wrinkling her nose.

"No, but I wouldn't complain if you did. Ready to go?"

She put her bag over her shoulder and nodded.

I waited until we were inside my truck to tell her what I'd wanted to say for several days.

"There's nothing between me and my ex-wife. I need you to know that."

"You don't have to explain anything to me, Holt."

I clenched the steering wheel as I drove, frustration making it hard to stay measured.

"I'm explaining because I want to. I like you. Andrea has been trying to get in touch with me for weeks, and she's not supposed to call unless it's important. The kids got to decide for themselves if they wanted to have phone calls with her and right now, they don't."

"I know it's not my business, but"

I couldn't stop myself from interrupting her. "It is your business, though. I trust you, and I'm an open book. Ask me anything you want."

"What did she want?"

I exhaled heavily. "She had a falling-out with the new guy. My accountant told me about a month ago that he got a call from the police in California about Andrea's new boyfriend taking off with pretty much all her money. The divorce settlement. He left her with their new baby and no one knows where he is."

"Oh my God."

"I only know about it because she kept using my accountant for her money after the divorce. But it doesn't affect me and the kids, so I don't really care."

"She wants you back, doesn't she?"

I pulled up to a red light and looked over at her, taking her hand. "I'd never even consider getting back with her. Never. We've been over for a long time."

"I like you, too. You know I do. But didn't we decide we can't date?"

I shook my head, a war raging inside of me. How was staying away from her the right thing when she made me feel so damn good?

"I know we talked about it, but"

"Keller offered me a job."

I glanced at her and then back at the road, my pulse kicking up. I didn't like the indecisive tone in her voice. It sounded like she was equating the job offer with our feelings for each other somehow.

"That's why I was with him at 3Bs," she said.

"A job as his personal chef? The one you've already turned him down for?"

"Yeah."

I parked at Taco Train, processing what she'd just

told me as I walked around to open her door. She'd already stepped out when I got there.

"You're thinking about it, aren't you?" I asked.

She shrugged. "I don't know...maybe?"

We walked into the restaurant, Shea nodding and waving at people she knew. It wasn't possible to continue our conversation until we were seated at a booth, a basket of chips and a bowl of salsa between us.

"What would that mean?" I asked her. "You'd work in his home all the time?"

"Don't tell anyone about this, okay? You're the only one I've told."

"I won't."

She nodded. "He wants me to travel with him, but he says he'd give me time off to make up for all the travel."

This couldn't happen. Whether we were together or not, I couldn't stand the thought of Shea being gone for weeks or months at a time. Off on Keller Strauss's yacht, serving him gourmet meals every time he snapped his fingers. She was better than that.

"I don't get why he's so hung up on you being his chef. Doesn't he already have one? Is he going to fire that person if you take the job?"

She looked away. "I don't know."

Fuck. Why had it taken me so long to put the pieces together? Panic coursed through me as I realized Keller's ulterior motive, followed swiftly by anger.

"He wants you in his kitchen and his bedroom," I said bitterly. "That smug bastard."

"I haven't given him an answer."

"No," I said, my possessiveness taking over. "The answer is no."

Our server approached with a grin. "Our special tonight is three steak tacos with a side of tots."

"I'll take that with a water," Shea said.

"I'll take the special with a Modelo," I said.

Once the server was gone, Shea met my gaze across the table.

"I thought I was proving something by working seven days a week," she said. "It became a competition with myself, finding a way to oversee every meal, every recipe, every special booking. But why? I'm missing out on...everything. If I take a day off, it turns into a huge drama with Caden. I love cooking and I'll never stop doing it, but I need a change."

I sank against the back of the booth, having a hard time thinking about anything but punching Keller Strauss in the face.

"Yeah, I mean...he's a billionaire. And he doesn't

have kids, so I guess he can give you more than I can."

Just saying it made my chest ache. No matter how hard I was falling for Shea, my kids had to come first.

"I don't care about his money. And I adore your kids. This isn't about that. It's about my job and how much I need to make a change. I didn't even realize how much I needed it until I had an entire weekend off. That weekend was..." Our eyes locked. "It was amazing. For me."

"For me, too."

"Did you tell the kids about their mom coming here?"

I exhaled hard, taking a sip from my beer that had been delivered. "No. The kids both saw counselors after she left and the three of us also did family therapy. All the therapists told me my kids need predictability and consistency. I didn't want them to think she might be moving here or something, and I can't have her telling them she wants to get back with me."

I stared out the window, facing the hard truth: my life was a hot mess. Shea was an incredible woman with no baggage, and she deserved better than what I had to give her right now.

"That sounds like the right call."

"Don't let Keller put you under his thumb," I said, aggravated. "Your job shouldn't be tied to being anyone's girlfriend."

"I'm thinking about my job situation in baby steps. Step one is whether or not I can bring myself to leave The Moose. It's a big part of who I am."

I shook my head. "I know it feels that way, but you'll be the same woman no matter where you work. You're a great chef and a supportive friend. Someone who cares about others. Your talent and personality don't belong to anyone but you."

She gave me a grateful look. "That means a lot, thank you."

Our food came and we both dug in, Shea's eyes widening as she took the first bite of a taco.

"Oh wow, I'd love to know what they marinated that in. It's so tender."

"Not quite as good as your steak, but I like it," I said with a wink.

She groaned. "Why are you so amazing?"

I couldn't let go of this feeling. It was a fullness inside every part of me that I only felt when I was with her.

"At least wait until after the wedding to give Keller an answer," I said. "I know we didn't solve anything tonight, but I think the more time you spend thinking about working for him, the more likely you are to realize it's the wrong decision."

"You mean to chicken out?" She laughed lightly.

"Don't think of it like you only have two options. You're an incredible chef."

"In a very small town," she countered.

"Promise me you'll wait until after the wedding."

"Promise."

Grady and Avon were tying the knot this weekend. That gave me a few days to think about things, too.

Though it was hard to think about anything but kissing Shea when she was directly across from me. And, of course, the occasional thought of knocking out Keller fucking Strauss.

CHAPTER EIGHTEEN

Shea

"Is my lipstick okay?" Avon turned to me with a questioning look.

It hit me in that moment. I'd seen her beautiful finished updo earlier and I'd helped her put on her beaded white gown with a halter neckline. When a makeup artist was applying her makeup, I was in the chair next to hers, getting my own makeup done.

But seeing it all come together like this—knowing that this woman I already loved, like a sister, was about to be my brother's wife—made me teary-eyed.

"You promised!" she said with a smile, waving a hand at her eyes. "No crying because then I'll cry and I don't want my makeup ruined."

"Sorry," I said, looking away from her and getting myself together. "You're right. Lipstick is good."

Poor Bess had burst into tears the moment she saw Avon in the dress, and she'd left the room several times so Avon wouldn't see her crying. It was understandable, though. This was a joyful day, but Avon's parents hadn't lived to see it. Her Uncle Don was walking her down the aisle.

If Avon's Uncle Pete hadn't passed away unexpectedly and left her the Sven's Beard Chronicle, none of us would be here right now. Grady and Avon never would have met. I couldn't imagine my brother with anyone else. He and Avon were a perfect match.

"Bridesmaids, assemble," the wedding planner Sean said.

My heart pounded as I took my place in line and Sean passed me a small bouquet of calla lilies. Someone brought Bess into the room, guiding her to her spot while she kept her head down.

It was funny. Bess was such a no-nonsense person, but she'd formed a bond with Avon. Avon had lost her parents, but she had a family again. Some of us related to her, and some of us did not. Family was more than just blood.

"I need new tissues," Bess said.

Sean passed her a fresh batch, which she

wrapped around the stems of her bouquet. She looked straight ahead, not chancing a glance at Avon as Don walked into the room.

"You ladies look beautiful," he said to the row of bridesmaids.

Avon chose simple sage-green dresses, letting everyone choose their own style. Mine was sleeveless with a long skirt, which had seemed like a good idea before my worries about tripping over the skirt on the way down the aisle had crept in.

"Absolutely stunning," Don said to Avon, kissing her on the cheek.

"Okay, ladies, it's time," Sean said. "Remember, *glide* down the aisle. No stomping. And go slowly. It's a wedding, not a relay race."

The wedding was on the lawn of The Sleepy Moose, which was the most beautiful spot in the Beard. We had to make a long walk from the room we'd gotten ready in, and I teared up again when I rounded a corner and saw guests on either side of the aisle, my brother beaming at the end as he waited for his bride.

Grady stood in front of an archway covered in brightly colored flowers, his groomsmen beside him. My gaze slid to Holt and I inhaled sharply when I saw him.

He cleaned up very well, his tux perfectly fitted

to him. But it was the way he was looking at me that made it hard to concentrate on slowly gliding. His eyes held reverence and hope.

The closer I got, the faster my heart raced. There was such irony in our situation. Holt's hesitation to date me only made me more attracted to him. He wanted to do right by his kids instead of jumping into something just for himself.

I had to look away so I didn't forget where I was going and walk straight up to Holt instead. I took my place next to Allie, who gave me an encouraging smile.

Karlsson Lake was shining in the background as Bess came down the aisle, tears streaming down her cheeks when she saw Grady.

When Avon came around the corner, I glanced at my brother and saw that he was about to cry, and I had to take a deep breath to keep it together. I reached for Bess's hand and squeezed it.

Once Avon was standing beside Grady, everyone focused their attention on them. All I had to do was look slightly past them to see Holt, and when I did, I found his gaze locked on me.

I promised him I'd wait until after the wedding to give Keller an answer, and I still had no idea which direction I wanted to go.

Being near Holt made me giddy. Hopeful.

Nervous. Joyful. I wanted us to be so much more than we were right now. But I respected his prioritizing his kids. It would be agonizing to be so close to him but to only be friends.

It would also be agonizing to be far away and never get to see him, Spencer and Marley.

I forced my attention back to Grady and Avon when he started reciting his vows.

"Avon..." His voice shook and he took a second to compose himself. "Shit, okay. Avon, you light up every room you walk into. You show people the best parts of themselves and everyone who knows you is better for it." He took a breath and wiped the corner of his eye. "You stand up taller and stronger than anyone I've ever known. I promise to love and honor you every day for the rest of my life. Everything I have and everything I am is yours now."

Avon beamed at him. I glanced at my mom, who had stars in her eyes. She held on to my dad's hand, sitting next to his wheelchair. Dad looked proud; this kind of happiness was everything he'd always hoped for his children to have.

"Ryan Grady, you are a force of nature," Avon said, smiling warmly as she began her vows. "You're the—" her voice wavered and she took a breath—"best man I've ever known. Beneath that gruff facade lies the most tender, caring and generous man who would help anyone in need. You make me proud every day. I promise you my heart forever. Whatever comes our way, in sickness or in health, I'll be by your side, always."

Bess passed me a tissue and I wiped the corners of my eyes. My gaze slipped to Holt, who put his hand over his heart. I wanted to drop my bouquet and run straight into his arms.

Grady kissed his bride, and when it was time for the bridal party to walk back down the aisle, it wasn't the groomsman who was supposed to be offering me his arm standing there, but Holt.

I put my arm through his, holding my skirt as we walked to avoid tripping. We'd made it almost all the way to the end when he leaned over to whisper in my ear.

"I had to know what it felt like to walk down the aisle with you."

My stomach did a full three-sixty rotation. "And? How was it?"

His expression turned serious. "Honestly? I think I might want to do it again at some point."

I tightened my hold on his arm, my knees weakening.

So, that really was a thing that happened outside of romance novels, and so was a man who checked all the boxes and then some.

THE BARN WAS DECORATED with white roses, lilies, and sage greenery. Lights twinkled inside glass hurricane centerpieces. After last night's rehearsal dinner, the wedding party had done all the decorating so Grady and Avon could spend time with out-of-town guests. Spencer and Marley had helped, Spencer never leaving my side.

The main cake was a masterpiece by Olivia from Sweets of Gold. It looked like a statue of Sven Karlsson, flowing red beard and all. I'd helped create secondary cakes for everyone to eat because fondant made for a spectacularly decorated cake, but it wasn't delicious.

The DJ turned on some music, a Taylor Swift song playing as I double-checked the food details with the caterers. Grady had initially been opposed to letting me do any sort of work on the reception food, but I'd talked him into letting me and Avon come up with the options and then hiring caterers to execute the plan.

"How are you keeping the roast beef warm?" I asked a white-uniformed member of the catering team.

"I have no idea. I'm just a server."

My anxiety about dried-out roast beef and cold potatoes was coming in hot.

"But did they tent the meat after they cooked it?" I asked.

I got a blank look in response.

"Okay, do you happen to know where Tom is?"

The head of the catering team could put my mind at ease. I'd given him specific written instructions, but it was always good to double-check.

"Never mind on that," a deep voice said from next to me.

I looked up to find Holt giving me an amused look, one brow arched.

"What's going on?" I asked.

"I'm under strict instructions from the bride not to let you oversee any aspect of the food."

I laughed lightly. "Well, I'm not really overseeing. I just want to check on a few things."

He shrugged, feigning innocence. "I don't argue with brides on their wedding day. I was told to hand you a glass of champagne and make sure you don't do anything but enjoy yourself."

The server left, and I accepted the glass Holt passed me.

"That's a check on the champagne," I said. "Now, how will I go about enjoying myself?"

The devilish look in his eyes gave me butterflies.

"I can think of a few ideas," he said in a low tone.

"Oh?" I looked around. "Where are the kids?"

"They left with my folks after the ceremony. For some reason, they think wedding receptions are boring."

I laughed. "It sounds like they might have gotten that idea from their dad."

"I mean, some wedding receptions are boring," he said, shrugging.

"Don't you love the long wait for the bride and groom to finish their photos and arrive? Everyone's eating peanuts and grumbling under their breath while pretending they don't care."

"Love that part."

"I made sure the servers would be walking around with appetizers while we waited. So you can thank me for *overseeing* that when you're eating a sausage on a stick."

He nudged me gently with his shoulder. "I'm gonna go ahead and plead guilty to having a one-track mind before I tell you I'd much rather watch *you* eat a sausage on a stick."

"I haven't eaten anything today, so you'll be seeing that very soon."

"Excellent."

I was about to ask Holt if he wanted to come with me to say hello to my parents when Keller

Strauss approached us, his gaze locked firmly on me.

"Shea, you look lovely," he said.

"Thanks."

I willed Grady and Avon to walk through the door immediately because an encounter between Holt and Keller wasn't likely to end well.

"Holt," Keller said, nodding at him.

"Keller."

"Can I get you a drink?" Keller asked me.

"She has a drink," Holt said.

Keller grinned at Holt like he was a pesky kid. "I meant a non-complimentary drink."

"Okay." Holt glanced away, clearing his throat. "Nice to see you, Keller. Enjoy the reception."

The two men just stared at each other, Keller not accepting the cue to walk away. I tipped back the last of the champagne and set my glass down.

"Really beautiful day for a wedding, isn't it?" I said. "Oh, here come the appetizers! Who's hungry?"

A server stopped and we all took fruit skewers and tiny sausages.

"Can we have the wedding party meet up outside?" the DJ asked. "It's almost time for the bride and groom to make their first entrance as Mr. and Mrs. Ryan Grady!"

"Shall we?" Holt offered me his arm.

I took it and we walked away, Keller fuming at the man he'd partnered with to build the youth hockey arena.

This was one wedding reception that would not be boring.

CHAPTER NINETEEN

Holt

I was done stealing the occasional glance at Shea. There was only one woman in this whole place I wanted to look at, and I wanted to look openly.

Even out on the dance floor doing the chicken dance with the other bridesmaids, she was glowing with happiness. This was the way she'd been on our weekend away—carefree and full of laughter.

Once again, I beat Keller to Shea when the song ended, giving her a questioning look. She smiled and put her arm around my neck, letting me pull her against me with an arm around her waist.

I really needed to tip the DJ for every slow song he played. Three to four minutes of having Shea in my arms, all to myself, was heaven on earth.

"Not a chicken dancer?" she asked in a teasing tone.

"Not when I can watch you chicken dance instead."

She laughed. "I haven't done that in years."

"I think you're incredible."

She arched her brows in amusement. "At the chicken dance?"

"At everything."

Her expression shifted, her gaze softening. "Likewise."

"Shea, can I have a word?"

I looked over and found Keller looking at Shea. He had brass balls. I had to give him that.

"No," I answered for her. "She's busy."

He gave me an irritated glance. "Why don't you let her answer for herself?"

Business partner or not, he needed to back the fuck off. He was trying to buy Shea's affection with his piles of money, and I wasn't going to just stand back and let it happen.

Shea gave him an apologetic look. "I'll catch up with you another time, okay?"

Keller nodded, not even looking at me again, before walking away. I pulled Shea closer, her chest against mine and her head against my shoulder.

When the song ended, the DJ announced that

Avon was going to throw her bouquet before she and Grady left to spend their wedding night at a secluded cabin about an hour from the Beard. They were flying to Hawaii tomorrow for a weeklong honeymoon.

Once all the single women had lined up, Avon tossed her bouquet, which Carmen lunged for. Shea met my eyes and shrugged.

After we said our goodbyes to Grady and Avon, I leaned in and spoke in Shea's ear.

"Come back to my room with me."

Her eyes widened. "Are you sure?"

"Completely. There's so much I wish I could promise you that I can't..." I cupped her cheek in my hand. "But tonight I can be all yours if that's what you want."

She nodded. "I do. But how about my place instead?"

My body heated in response to her suggestion, hunger and certainty swirling in her eyes as they locked onto mine. Would one night satisfy the ache I felt for her or intensify it?

I didn't want to waste another minute seeking the answer to that question. We said a few more quick goodbyes and were soon in my truck on the way to her house.

"Are you nervous?" she asked me.

"I wouldn't call it nervous... Excited, I guess. What about you?"

"Both."

I put a hand on her knee. "You've got nothing to be nervous about."

"How many women have you been with?"

I hesitated, hoping my answer wouldn't change her view of me. "Two."

"Oh wow. That makes me feel a lot better."

I laughed lightly. "You thought I was a manwhore?"

"Well, that's what I get for assuming...I just thought you'd say a much higher number."

"What's your number?"

"It's, uh...it's three."

"All of them damn lucky," I said.

I parked in her driveway, which in the Beard was like a neon sign announcing we were spending the night together.

Shea gave me a questioning look and I said, "Let 'em talk."

Her eyes shone with happiness when I met her on the passenger side of the truck and took her hand. We walked around to the side entry door and she took out a key ring, unlocking the door.

As soon as we stepped inside, she closed the door

and shoved something from the kitchen counter into the sink.

"Try not to notice the laund"

I cut her off by pulling her into my arms and kissing her. Finally, we were alone. We'd never truly been alone. Not at the cabin when everyone else was inside eating, and definitely not at the reception when we'd been surrounded by people.

But now, at last, I could kiss her the way I wanted to. She dropped her bag to the ground and kissed me back, wrapping her arms around my neck.

We kissed each other in front of her kitchen sink until we were both breathless. She tugged my dress shirt out of my pants and started unbuttoning it, my tie long gone already.

"Can I unzip this?" I asked, my fingers pausing on the zipper of her gown.

"Um, I actually have a shapewear situation happening. Can we go into the bedroom?"

"Yeah, of course."

I wasn't sure what a shapewear situation was, and I didn't ask. I undressed down to my boxers as Shea went into her walk-in closet and when she came back out, she was only wearing a lacy white bra and panties, her expression shy and lusty at the same time.

"Holy fuck," I said as I took in her nearly naked body. "You're so sexy."

She got in bed and I followed, leaning on an elbow as I kissed her neck and chest, my hand on her thigh. It had been so long since a woman had touched me as tenderly as she did; my body froze at first and then heated all over.

"I've wanted this for so long," she said softly. "You know I had a hard-core crush on you in high school, right?"

My eyes widened in shock. "You did?"

"Me and half the female student population at Sven's Beard High School, Holt," she said with a warm smile.

"I wish I'd known."

"My brother would have literally murdered you."

I arched a brow. "He's still contemplating it."

She slid a hand inside my boxers and I groaned.

"I'll try my best to make it worth dying for," she quipped.

I took her by the wrist and then captured her other one in my free hand, pinning them above her head. She inhaled sharply, her chest rising and falling as she breathed.

"I get you first," I said, kissing her.

She moaned softly as I slid her bra straps off her shoulders and eased the cups of her bra down, taking my time licking and sucking each of her nipples.

Every taste of her was bliss. The feel of her body chased away every doubt inside me. This was right. We were made for each other.

I pulled her panties off, enjoying every moan and gasp as I explored every inch of her. She was responsive, her back arching off the bed as I worshiped her with my mouth.

"I want you," she said, her voice strangled with desire. "I want you inside me, Holt."

"I don't have condoms," I said, panic seizing my chest.

What a rookie fucking mistake. Why hadn't I bought condoms?

Shea opened her legs wider and said, "I'm on birth control. Don't stop."

It was music to my ears. As soon as I entered her, our groans mingled and everything in me demanded more, more, more.

We found a rhythm, our bodies perfectly fitted. Her breasts bounced with every thrust, testing my self-control. It had been so long and she felt so damn good.

"God," she breathed. "Yes."

I slowed down, needing to prolong our first time. It couldn't be our only time. This was too perfect, a sonata meant to be played again and again.

She moved her hips in time with mine, making me go faster. I loved how eager she was, and while I planned to show her how incredible teasing could feel, I didn't want to do it now.

We climbed together, her reaching a peak first and crying out my name when she did. The sound of my name on her lips and the way she clenched around me sent me over the edge and I came with a powerful groan, my lips an inch from hers.

"Wow," she said, breathless as I moved off of her. "That was wow."

"It was wow," I agreed. "Your body is incredible."

She laughed lightly. "You mean my Jell-O tummy or my saggy rear?"

"I mean all of it. Your big sexy tits and your ass I just want to take a bite out of. I get hard just looking at you."

"Really?"

"Yeah, and it's pretty inconvenient sometimes. Can you stop being so hot?"

She rolled onto her side and kissed me. "You make me feel so good. No one has ever made me feel as good as you do."

I felt about ten feet tall. There was no greater compliment than that.

"You make me feel good, too. And happy."

I kissed her and she snuggled against me. "You seem like you're always in a good mood. Are you?"

"I try to be. Attitude is everything. But we all have bad days."

"This was an amazing day," she said softly.

"I couldn't agree more."

"Are you hungry? I could whip something up."

I put an arm around her waist. "I'm not hungry for food. You're not leaving this bed anytime soon."

She hummed her amusement. "Promises, promises. I hear hockey players don't have much stamina."

I laughed because the opposite was true. I loved the way Shea poked fun at me.

"Challenge accepted," I said, moving back on top of her. "Good luck walking tomorrow."

Her giggle was stifled by my kiss. This was the culmination of every sexual fantasy I'd had since moving back home—every one of them about her.

We wouldn't be getting much sleep tonight.

CHAPTER TWENTY

Shea

I pushed the covers aside and sat up, finding Holt sitting on the small bench at the foot of my bed, tying his dress shoes. He turned and smiled softly.

"Sorry I woke you up."

I took a few seconds to silently admire him. His dress shirt was unbuttoned at the neck and his sandy hair was a sexy mess. The light coating of scruff on his face was a shade darker than his hair.

"It's okay," I said, suddenly self-conscious.

It was a good thing I'd pulled on a T-shirt before finally going to bed in the wee hours of the morning. I'd never slept naked and I never would. Too many worst-case scenarios about firefighters unexpectedly seeing me naked ran through my head.

"I'll make us some breakfast," I said, sliding out of bed.

Holt stood, stuffing his tie into his pants pocket. "Actually, I told my parents I'd meet them and the kids at Tipper's."

"Okay, no problem."

"You should go back to sleep. It's only seven. I have to go back to The Moose and take a shower."

Right. He couldn't show up for breakfast in a rumpled tuxedo. I felt a surge of guilt over last night. Like what we'd done was somehow illicit.

"Can I get a ride back to The Barn to get my car?" I asked as I pulled on a pair of jean shorts. "If you have time."

"Of course."

He came over and put his arms around me, his hands on my ass giving me tingles of awareness and arousal. My hips were sore from last night, but every inch of me still wanted more.

"Last night was incredible," he said, kissing each of my cheeks, my forehead and the tip of my nose before brushing his lips over mine.

His warmth and affection made my guilt slip away. "It was."

He rested his forehead against mine. "I wish I could spend the whole day with you."

"Me too."

I smiled as he kissed my jawline, making his way down to my neck. His neck kisses gave me goose bumps every time. I wanted more, not just of the kissing, but of him.

More than he could give me.

"This is hard," I said softly.

He sighed and held me close. "I know."

I wasn't going to cry. I made myself hold back my tears because I knew the deal before I spent the night with him.

One night. He couldn't promise me more than that. I gently pushed myself away from him and forced a smile.

"I'm just going to change shirts real quick and get my shoes on so I can go in to work once I get my car."

"On a Sunday?"

I laughed lightly. "People be wanting to eat on Sundays, too."

"Why don't you show up at Tipper's right after me? Then you can join us for breakfast."

It was a nice offer, but it made me feel weird. I couldn't pretend I just happened to be there at the same time, planning to eat breakfast alone until I saw Holt and his family. His parents would see right through that.

"I need to go to work," I said, walking toward

my bathroom. "Just give me five minutes to get ready."

Once we were in his truck on the way to The Barn, he gave me a concerned look. "You okay?"

"Yeah, I'm good."

That was mostly true. I didn't regret last night, but I hadn't expected to feel so weird about things this morning. Holt and I had now checked every box he was able to check: dinner out, a weekend with heavy flirting at a cabin and a hot postwedding night of sex.

What was left?

"Did I look better after several glasses of champagne than I do this morning?" he teased.

He actually looked better to me this morning with his messy hair and rumpled dress shirt. It felt intimate, a snapshot of a moment I'd always treasure.

"You look great as always," I said as I looked out the passenger window at the houses we passed.

"Talk to me, Shea." He reached over and put a hand on my knee. "What's wrong?"

I shrugged. "I'm okay, really. Probably just tired."

"I wish I didn't have to leave first thing, but I promised the kids I'd be there for breakfast."

I looked over at him. "Hey, you don't need to apologize. We both knew the deal going in."

He furrowed his brow. "Yeah, but...that wasn't a one-night stand."

I covered his hand with my own, speaking out loud the things I couldn't seem to get straight in my own mind.

"I like you a lot, but I don't want to be any man's secret lover. I wish you were at a point where you're ready for a relationship, but"

"I'm ready. I just don't want my kids to feel insecure."

"And I get that and I respect it. I want to be your friend, and I want to be a friend to your kids. But this is a small town, and if we try to see each other and keep it from your kids, it will come back to bite us in the ass. They'll hear about it. I don't want that."

He stared out the windshield, his jaw set in a tense line. "I don't want to lose you. Not to Keller or any other man."

We'd arrived at The Barn and he pulled up next to my car, putting his truck in park.

"Look," I said, turning to face him. "I don't know what the future holds. I've decided to tell Keller that if he needs an answer immediately on the job offer, the answer is no. I need more time to explore my options. I've been thinking about what you said about there being more than just two job choices for me. I don't have the bandwidth to start my own restaurant because that would take as much time or more than The Moose takes now. But I'm thinking. And while I think, I'm staying in the Beard." I took his hand and squeezed it. "So be my friend. Move into your new house and get going with your new job. Let's see where things stand in a few months."

He nodded, his expression forlorn.

"So you're still considering working for Keller?"

I shrugged. "Maybe? I don't know. I never thought I'd work anywhere but The Moose, so I'm trying to take my time thinking things through."

"Okay."

"Hey," I said softly. "Last night was amazing. Let's not feel like we need an answer for every question right now."

He cupped my cheek in his palm and we both leaned in, meeting in the middle for a kiss. I didn't know if I was feeling my own longing not to get out of the truck and leave or his longing for me to stay. But, like all good things, our magical night together had to come to an end.

"Enjoy your breakfast," I said softly.

"Don't work too hard."

I smiled at him as I got out of the truck, trying to make my expression light, though my heart was heavy.

I wouldn't be a woman who put pressure on a single dad to give me more than he was ready for. It wasn't how I was made. But deep down inside, I could admit to myself that I'd never wanted more with any man as much as I wanted it with Holt.

CHAPTER TWENTY-ONE

Holt

"Up and at 'em!" I flipped the light switch and both kids groaned. "It's moving day, offspring! Let's get going."

Spencer, true to form, sat up and put his glasses on. Marley, also true to form, pulled the covers over her head, refusing to get up.

"I guess we'll have to find some other kid to give Marley's room to," I said loudly.

"Can we?" Spencer asked hopefully.

I gave him a look.

"I don't want to leave," Marley said, her voice muffled by the covers.

"You have a cool new canopy bed at the house, peanut. The movers set it up yesterday. You're gonna love it."

"I like it here."

I sat down at the end of her bed. "You want to stay in these two rooms at The Moose forever?"

"Yes."

"We like it here, Dad," Spencer said. "We get to see Shea and all our other friends all the time. We'll never see them when we live in the house."

His mention of Shea shook me because I had the same worry. No more run-ins or evenings on the lawn. The closer the two of us got, the more I missed her when we went several days at a time without seeing each other.

"People come and go from here, guys," I said. "The friends you have who are staying here this summer won't be here forever, either."

"Shea's not leaving," Spencer said glumly.

I rubbed my forehead, trying not to think about the amount of money I spent building the house my kids felt no enthusiasm for.

"Our kayaks are at the house. We can go out on the lake anytime we want now. You guys will have your own rooms again. We have that cool ice cream machine you guys wanted so much in the kitchen."

"Can I still go to adventure camp with Marina?" Marley asked, still beneath the covers.

"Uh...no, that's for inn guests only, but we can

make our own adventure camp. We have lots of woods at the new house, or we can go to the farm."

Spencer came out of the bathroom, dressed and ready to go already. "We can eat breakfast here, right?"

"Right. And I bet we'll be able to find another kid to take Marley's room while we're there." I walked over to the door. "Bye Marley!"

"No, I'm coming!"

She scrambled out of bed, grabbed clean clothes and ran to the bathroom to change.

"So we're eating, then packing up the room, then heading for the new house," I told them before opening the door.

"I need to see Shea before we go," Spencer said.

Same. I ruffled my son's hair. "She said you can stop by the kitchen anytime."

As soon as we got to a table in the dining hall, Spencer went to see Shea. It was painful knowing she was so close and I probably wouldn't get to see her today, but I was glad he'd have a chance to say goodbye.

Marley and I ordered drinks and were discussing a sleepover she wanted to have for a friend she'd made in my parents' neighborhood when Spencer returned, grinning from ear to ear.

"Shea's making us a special breakfast," he said.

"We're having churro pancakes and bacon and...I forgot the other stuff."

Marley beamed at me. "Churro pancakes are my favorite."

"That's why she's making them," Spencer said.

The director of children's activities at The Moose, Marina, came to our table to hug the kids goodbye. Guests we'd gotten to know stopped by, too, and I had to remind a tearful Marley that none of them would be staying here forever, either.

Our summer in the bubble of The Sleepy Moose was everything we needed. I was ready to live in a full-sized house again and have more than one bathroom, but I was also going to miss the people here.

One in particular. Shea brought our breakfast out herself, a server following behind her with the dishes she couldn't carry.

For Marley, she'd made churro pancakes with whipped cream and a side of bacon. Spencer got the same with a side of the fresh mango he loved. My plate had an omelet prepared exactly how I liked it: with spinach, tomatoes, sausage and cheddar. Crispy hash browns and wheat toast completed my plate.

"No shellfish," she told Spencer with a grin.

"This looks amazing," I said. "All of our favorites. Thank you."

"We've loved having your family here this

summer. And we wish you a wonderful moving day."

I met her gaze, missing the intimacy we'd shared. She was the chef at The Sleepy Moose right now, and I wanted Shea, the woman who was ticklish and got tipsy off of a single drink.

There was a softness in her eyes that gave me a glimpse of that side of her, but it passed quickly. I tried not to be alarmed, but how could I not be? All I wanted was to tell Shea how much I wanted her, and instead, we'd taken a step back at her insistence.

She bent down next to Spencer. "Thank you again for my present. I love it so much."

He smiled at her through a bite of pancakes. "You're welcome."

She kissed him on the forehead and I felt a warm sensation in my chest. Spencer thought he had outgrown affection years ago, but he didn't seem to mind it from Shea.

"Marley, can I have a hug?" she asked.

Marley got up and approached Shea, wrapping her arms around Shea's waist and looking up at her.

"Do you want to come to my sleepover?"

It was all I could do not to look at Shea. A sleepover sounded like a damn good idea to me.

"I...might," Shea said, clearly caught off guard. "But for now, I have to get back to the kitchen."

She turned to leave and Spencer said, "Hey, what

about Dad?"

"What do you mean?" Shea asked, looking at me.

"You didn't say goodbye to Dad."

Her expression softened and she walked over to me. "Well, we can't have that."

My pulse pounded as I hugged her, the familiar coconut scent of her shampoo making me wish for more than a hug.

"Thanks for this," I said in her ear.

"You're welcome."

I reluctantly released her and she held my gaze for a couple of seconds before turning to go. Instinct told me to chase after her, to not let go of the best woman I'd ever known because the timing was off.

I didn't, though. Instead, I watched her walk back to the kitchen, not sitting back down until the door had closed behind her.

"Shea is beautiful," Spencer said.

"Yes, she is."

I wasn't sure who was crazier about Shea—me or my son. But I had a feeling I was going to be the one who missed her the most.

———

"YOUR UTENSIL DRAWER should always be close to the dishwasher," my mom said that evening as she unloaded cutlery from a kitchen drawer.

"You know more than I do about that stuff, so rearrange anything you want," I said. "I'm ordering the pizza soon. What do you guys like on yours?"

"If you're ordering from Northern Lights, we like Sven's Special."

"I love that place, but I'm just curious. Does any other place deliver?"

"No, but the Kirby's gas station has delicious pizza and it's a lot cheaper than Northern Lights if you don't mind picking it up."

My parents had refused every financial gift I'd ever tried to give them. They were too proud to accept it, preferring to pay their own way. I knew they were financially secure, but I still wished they'd let me help out.

"I'll remember that," I said.

"Grandma, let's read stories," Marley said as she walked into the kitchen.

My mom put down the forks in her hand. "I'm on my way, granddaughter!"

I'd built a massive house with six bedrooms. We each had a bedroom, there were two guest rooms, and the kids had a shared space with a castle built into one wall that served as a play area and reading nook for now, pillows covering the floor inside the castle. The builder had designed that room to be converted into a study room when the kids got older.

Our basement had a theater room, a game room and a room for my hockey memorabilia. The main level was open, smelling of fresh-cut wood and painted light gray with white woodwork.

I wanted to show it to Shea. I wanted to sit with her in the rocking chairs on my deck and hear about her day while we watched the sun setting over the lake.

"You look lost in thought," my dad said, putting a hand on my shoulder.

"Just thinking about everything it took to get here."

He nodded, the lines in his face etched deeper than before, but his eyes were still full of the wisdom I'd always admired in him. My dad was a rock; nothing threw him for a loop. Or if it did, he never let it show.

"You know how proud I was of your career," he said. "I can only imagine the amount of commitment it takes to play at that level for more than a decade. But I've never been more proud than I was on the day you retired."

Emotion flooded my chest; my dad was always supportive but rarely emotional.

"You've made your kids number one for a year

now," he said. "And look at them, they're thriving."

I nodded. "I hope so. I know I've done my best."

"You know it's okay if you don't want to live here alone with them until they're adults, right? To want someone in your life again? That just means you've gotten enough distance from what happened with Andrea that you're ready to move on."

I knew he'd heard about me and Shea. Word spread fast in the Beard and we'd spent Grady and Avon's entire wedding night in each other's arms on the dance floor.

"When will I know if my kids are ready, though?"

My dad smiled. "You'll know. Just don't overcompensate for what their mom did. Never being with a woman because she left for another man doesn't prove anything. Martyrdom is a lonely pursuit, son."

"I'm not trying to be a martyr," I said, furrowing my brow in thought. "Is that what it seems like?"

"It seems like you're giving up everything for them just to cover all your bases. But don't throw out the baby with the bathwater."

After a few seconds of silent thought, I sighed heavily. "It's hard to imagine trusting someone again. I had no idea what was going on with Andrea."

"Don't fault someone else for what she did. Life's too short for that."

I looked up at the vaulted ceiling in the great

room, covered with wood planks. This house was very different from the cozy three-bedroom ranch I'd grown up in. Mom had always had something baking in the oven and we'd all gathered around the same TV to watch a show on our free evenings. There were definitely no castles. But home had been my safe place, and I loved it.

"You think this place feels like a home?" I asked my dad.

"Oh, I imagine it will. The kids will make it feel like one."

"You know you guys are welcome here anytime. Don't let Mom sell you on having to be invited. I want you guys here."

He gave me a knowing smile. "I don't think a lack of an invitation will keep her from our grandkids."

"Good."

"And you know, we're damn good babysitters. When you need us. We love having them overnight."

"Thanks, Dad."

He nodded. "Be a shame to sit in one of those rockers by yourself every day, you know. Some things are just better in pairs."

It was eerie how well he knew me. I hoped one day I'd know my kids that well and that I'd steer them in the right direction when they needed it—whether they asked me to or not.

CHAPTER TWENTY-TWO

Shea

"Where is the gravy?"

I'd asked nicely twice; now I was yelling. I had seven plates of beef Wellington, garlic mashed potatoes and roasted veggies that were cooling by the second. I refused to use warming lamps in my kitchen because they made cooks lazy.

"Sorry, Chef." Priscilla hurried over to ladle gravy onto the mashed potatoes on each plate.

"Everything okay?" I asked her because she was always someone I could count on to have her jobs done on time.

She gave me a frantic look. "Nothing I can't handle."

"What is it?"

"Marie has a nut allergy. She can't be in the

kitchen tonight because of the slivered almonds on the green beans., so I put her on dishes."

I looked over at Priscilla's station, frustration building hard and fast when I didn't see Marie there. Our newest employee was supposed to be backing up Priscilla tonight, which was why I'd assigned Priscilla work for two people instead of one.

"Damn, I'm sorry. You should have told me."

"Just rolling with it during the rush, Chef."

It was something I asked my seasoned employees to do: roll with the unexpected when things were crazy busy. I told them we'd sort out the details when things slowed down.

"You're the best," I said. "Ask Charlie to take over on toasting almonds."

"I've got it. I'll tell you if I need help."

I nodded, watching as servers left with the plates of beef Wellington. It was one of the most expensive dishes we sold here at The Moose and always one of the most popular.

Nina nodded at me from the beef Wellington station, reading my mind. She knew I *always* asked prospective employees about allergies. Marie had assured me she had none.

Knowing the beef was in good hands, I walked into the back room, where Marie was rinsing dishes and loading them into industrial-sized dishwashers.

"Hey, do you have any allergies?" I asked.

"Oh." She grinned at me like I'd just told a hilarious joke. "Yeah. I thought if I told you that during the interview, you wouldn't hire me."

It wasn't the right time for a conversation, but she couldn't be employed here full time, which put me in a huge bind. I'd struggled all summer to find kitchen help for the low wages Caden required we pay here.

"I actually can't have you on dishes, either," I said. "There could be nuts on the dirty dishes. You'll need to clock out."

"Clock out? But I have a five-hour shift."

I put a palm up. "You should have told me about your allergy."

"Why, so you could discriminate against me? This is so unfair."

I'd been in a bad mood since Holt and his kids left the inn four days ago, and I didn't need any more fuel added to the flames.

"I'm going to clock you out," I told Marie. "Leave the apron in here and do not walk back into the kitchen for any reason."

"Am I fired?" she called as I walked away.

"I'll see if there's another job for you at the inn outside of the kitchen, but you can't work in here."

The double doors closed behind me and I took a deep breath, walking back over to Nina.

"Did you have a broken butane torch on your bingo card for tonight?" she asked me.

"Are you fucking joking?"

She gave me a look. "Do you know me? Would I try to crack a joke right now?"

I laughed maniacally. The backup torch was broken, too. This job was fifty percent cooking and fifty percent problem-solving.

"Broil the crème brûlée," I called out to the dessert station. "There are instructions in the blue binder."

"We're having fun though, right?" Nina said. "And I heard no one's getting a raise again this year so that just adds to it."

I stopped in the middle of wiping down our stainless workstation. "What?"

"Joanna, in housekeeping, said day shift was told today before their shifts started. They gave everyone a coffee mug to thank them for their hard work. What a joke."

I said nothing, but inside I was seething. As the chef and the head of a department at The Sleepy Moose, I was part of budget meetings and I knew how much profit this place made. Caden had promised me last month that everyone who had worked in the kitchen for at least six months would be getting a five percent raise.

I told myself not to jump to conclusions. Maybe it was just housekeeping that wasn't getting raises, not that it was fair to give anyone the shaft. The Sleepy Moose had broken revenue records in the past year. Raises were always given out in early fall to keep people motivated to work hard during our busiest season. The owners of The Moose lived in California and had bought the inn as an investment. If they stiffed the employees, I had a major problem with locals giving so much of themselves to work here.

But again, I told myself, it might not be true. I couldn't react based on a rumor I'd heard.

"I'll get the beef. You get the ham, mushrooms and pastry," I told Nina.

"You got it, boss."

Holt was a huge fan of my beef Wellington. He'd ordered it every night it was on the menu during his stay. I imagined he and I were alone in my kitchen, talking and sipping on drinks as I made this meal just for the two of us.

He'd told me several times that if he were stranded on an island and only able to eat one thing for the rest of his life, it would be my garlic mashed potatoes. He joked that he'd be the reverse of the movie *Castaway*—a guy who gained weight on the island from eating a plateful of mashed potatoes for three meals a day.

I missed the way he raved over my food. He would send notes to the kitchen with his server, sometimes telling me how many stars he and the kids gave their meals, and he always signed them with the letter *H* instead of his full name.

"You okay, chef?" Nina asked me as we set ingredients on the prep table.

"Yeah, why?"

She shrugged. "You had a faraway look in your eyes."

"Probably because I wish I was far away from here," I cracked.

"Beef Wellington keeps us on our toes. Meanwhile, my kids are at home having microwaved hot dogs and they think that's fine dining."

My anger over the raises resurfaced. Nina could have been at home with her kids, but she was here making filet mignon wrapped in pastry for people with more disposable income than she'd ever have.

As soon as the dinner rush died down, I was going to find Caden.

———

"Is it urgent?" Caden asked when I approached him in the lobby a couple of hours later.

"It is."

"Mr. and Mrs. Hawthorne, welcome back to The Sleepy Moose," he said to a couple passing by. "Please let me know if I can make your stay more enjoyable in any way."

"Do we need to go into my office?" Caden asked me.

"We do."

He offered his fake smile to passing guests as we walked, my anger simmering slowly. If it boiled over, I wanted us to be alone.

"I got many compliments on the beef Wellington tonight," my boss said as we walked into his office.

"That's great," I said, closing the door behind me. "Is the kitchen staff still getting the five percent raise you promised me a month ago?"

He gave me the same smarmy smile he gave our guests. "Aaron wasn't supposed to tell the house-keeping staff about their performance awards for two more weeks."

"What performance awards? Why wasn't I part of this conversation?"

He sat down, gesturing at a chair in front of his desk. I shook my head, arms crossed, as I glared at him.

"I met with Mike and Angela last week, and we set some benchmarks. I decided to meet with each department head privately about it. I know you're swamped right now, so"

Mike and Angela were the owners, and they were notoriously disinterested in meeting anyone who worked here. They ran this place only for the money. The day the local man who built The Sleepy Moose sold it was a sad one.

"Just answer my question," I said. "On the raises. Yes or no?"

Caden folded his hands on his desk. "We've decided to approach things differently. For the next year, we're going to set performance-based benchmarks for every department."

"Yes or no, Caden? It's not that hard."

He gave me a stern look. "I don't like your tone, Shea."

He didn't like my tone? I wanted to burst into frustrated, angry laughter.

"Like you said, I'm very busy. I don't have time to stand here and listen to your doublespeak. Raises— yes or no?"

"You are getting a raise, which I planned to discuss in your performance review next month."

"And the kitchen staff?" I demanded.

"All non-department-head staff members are

getting a performance gift and an opportunity to earn a bonus next year."

I was on the edge of losing it. He had promised me. Raises were my only way of rewarding my people for long hours and a work environment that was, at times, stressful.

"What is the performance gift?"

Caden at least had the good sense to look sheepish. "It's a very nice coffee mug."

"Are you serious?" I roared. "After the year we've had"

My boss stood up, cutting me off. "Shea, you are not privy to all the financials of this business. This information can't leave this room, but Mike and Angela plan to add on a huge indoor pool with waterslides and it's going to cost a fortune. They can't do that *and* hand out five percent raises to everyone."

"Are you getting a raise?"

He scoffed, his eyes widening. "That's none of your business."

"Caden, I can go into my office and look at the budget anytime I want. Are you getting a raise?"

"I work harder than anyone here, Shea. And yes, I am getting a raise. Just like you are."

I was seeing red at this point.

"Nina has four kids. My dishwasher left because

he got a better-paying job at a gas station. I can't ask people to bend over backward for a place that doesn't value them."

Caden shrugged. "The performance bonus opportunity will allow them to earn a bonus of up to two thousand dollars."

I blew out a breath, my anger dissipating. He'd made this decision so easy for me.

"You can keep your raise and your shitty coffee mug and your bullshit performance bonus opportunity because I quit."

He gaped at me.

"Do you want me to work out a two-week notice, or should I leave now?"

"I...Shea, I can't possibly replace you in two weeks."

I shrugged. "Either I leave now, or I work out the two weeks. Which do you want?"

His shoulders sagged as reality set in. "Work out the two weeks."

I turned for the door, then spun around to face him. "You're a shitty boss and a horrible leader. It's gross to give yourself a raise when you already make so much and the people who scrub the toilets and wash the dishes here make so little. Do their jobs for one day and see how hard you think your job is then."

"Are you done?" he asked, a bitter edge to his tone.

"I am *so* done."

I left his office feeling lighter than I had in a long time.

CHAPTER TWENTY-THREE

Holt

"I need a four-letter word for a quick look," my dad said from the table and chairs on my deck.

"I've got some four-letter words for you," I quipped.

"Peep," my mom suggested.

"Nope."

"Hmm," she said, considering. "Peek?"

"Nope."

"Dad, look what we found!" Spencer cried, running from the yard onto the deck with something in his hand.

Marley was right behind him, her bare feet covered in dirt. Spencer opened his hand to reveal a little green critter whose world had just been upended.

"Hey, it's a frog," I said. "Go put him back so he doesn't die."

"Take a picture of him, Daddy," Marley said. "His name is Franco."

I took out my phone and snapped a photo. "Okay, now go put Franco back."

"Or you could kiss him and see if he turns into a prince," my mom suggested.

Marley wrinkled her nose. "Daddy, you kiss him."

"I'm gonna pass."

"Dad doesn't want a prince. He wants a princess," Spencer said.

"Maybe it's a girl frog," Marley suggested.

I pretended to consider it. "Are you thinking like a quick peck or a long kiss with tongue?"

Marley giggled. "Tongue. Do it, Daddy."

"That's gross, Dad," Spencer said. "You should kiss Shea instead."

I looked at him, my lips parted with surprise. Had he overheard something he shouldn't have?

"Why would you say that?" I asked.

He gave me an annoyed look. "It's so obvious you like her. Just kiss her."

My dad laughed, his eyes still locked onto his crossword puzzle. I looked at my mom, who was clearly amused, a smile playing on her lips.

"Maybe she wants to kiss you, too," Marley said.

Damn, I hoped so. I'd been so preoccupied with worry that she'd accept the job with Keller and leave town with him before I saw her again.

"But...how would you guys feel about me kissing her?" I asked.

Spencer shrugged. "Fine. She's really nice."

"Can I hold Franco?" Marley asked her brother.

"No, you'll squish him."

"I will not! Let me hold him."

"Marley, how would you feel about me dating someone?" I asked, surprised by Spencer's nonchalant reaction.

"I want Shea to come over and play with me and she can kiss you sometimes. Like when we take a break."

I looked at my mom, who shrugged and smiled encouragingly. "You won't find any finer people than the Gradys. I vote for you to kiss her."

"Grandpa, what about you?" Spencer asked.

"Scan!" he said, filling the letter in on his crossword before looking up at us. "I think life's much better when you have a beautiful woman to kiss. I know mine has been."

My mom walked over to him and kissed him. I hated to think about my parents doing anything more than kissing but judging by the look on my mom's face, Dad was definitely getting more than that tonight.

I needed to get to The Sleepy Moose as soon as possible. Hopefully my parents could stay and hang with the kids.

"Hey, can"

"Of course," my mom said. "Take all the time you need."

The kids were already gone, returning the frog to wherever they'd found it. I did a quick pit sniff, then ran to the bathroom to put on deodorant and brush my teeth.

I was full of nervous energy as I pulled out of my driveway. This was crazy, but it also wasn't.

What I felt for Shea was steady and certain. She could excite me or calm me, depending on the situation. I loved that she was a natural caregiver, and I wanted to show her that she deserved to be cared for, too.

She wanted us to stay friends and see how things were in a few months, but I couldn't do that. I needed to tell her how I felt now. Hopefully I wasn't too late. She'd said she wasn't accepting Keller's offer immediately, but with his deep pockets, he could have convinced her otherwise.

I parked at The Sleepy Moose, jogging through the front entrance, when someone called my name.

"Holt Sellers?"

I stopped to find a middle-aged man in a Minnesota Mammoths T-shirt staring at me with his mouth wide open.

"Oh my God, it is! It's you!" He put a hand on the shoulder of the little boy standing next to him. "Keaton, this is Holt Sellers, one of the greatest Mammoths ever to play the game."

I shook his hand, not letting on what a hurry I was in.

"It's great to meet you," I said.

"Kerry, I'm Kerry Sanders. I can't believe this! I was at the game when you broke the record for goals scored by a Mammoth at home."

What a night that had been. My teammates had poured so much champagne on my head that the janitorial staff had to bring in wet/dry vacuums to clean it up.

"That's awesome, man. I appreciate you."

"Hey, do you have a second for a picture with me and my son?"

"Of course."

We posed for several pictures and I signed an autograph on the only paper he could find, which was a gas station receipt.

"How long are you here for?" I asked.

"Four nights. My wife's cousin is getting married

here this weekend."

"I have to run right now, but leave your number at the front desk for me and we can get together for a drink."

"Holy shit! Okay!" He pumped my hand again. "Thanks!"

"Great to meet you guys," I said with a wave. "Bye, Keaton."

I resumed my jog to the front desk, where the clerk, Addison, greeted me with a smile.

"Mr. Sellers, welcome back. What can I do for you?"

"I need to see Shea Grady. Can I go back to the kitchen?"

Addison lowered her brows. "Shea quit. Do you want me to see if I can find a number for her?"

I exhaled heavily, defeat crushing me. It was the realization of my worst fear—Keller had sweet-talked her into working for him. This was all my fault. If I hadn't been so hesitant, Shea wouldn't have felt like she needed to step back, and Keller wouldn't have had the chance to steal her away.

"Hey Carl, do you happen to have a phone number for Shea Grady?" Addison said into the phone, pausing. "Because there's someone here who wants to talk to her." Another pause. "Oh, okay. Thanks."

She hung up the phone. "She's still here. You can go back to the kitchen."

I let out a single note of laughter, my emotions riding a roller coaster. "She's here?"

"Yeah, she's working out a two-week notice."

I pushed away from the desk. "Thanks."

Had she given notice because she was going to work for Keller? If so, I was going to do everything in my power to stop her. The timing wasn't perfect for us to go all in on a relationship, but I no longer cared.

I walked quickly, not wanting to knock anyone over, and when I finally made it to the kitchen, Shea was standing alone at the island, rolling something out with a rolling pin.

"Holt," she said, surprised.

"I'm in love with you."

She released her hold on the rolling pin, giving me a confused smile.

"Don't work for Keller," I said as I approached her. "Stay here and be with me. And my kids. I'm a package deal, but you know that."

She put a palm on my chest. "I told Keller I can't accept the job with him."

I frowned, confused. "But Addison just said you quit your job here."

"I did."

"But you're not leaving the Beard?"

"No. This is my home. I don't know what I'll do now, work-wise, but that doesn't matter. Can we get back to the part about you being in love with me?"

I took her hand. "I am. And I was a fucking idiot for not telling the entire world until now. I thought my kids would be bothered about it, but they adore you and...I guess it was all in my head. All the worries."

Tears glistened in her eyes. "So what are you saying?"

"I want you to be with me. Be my girlfriend, for now. Fuck the job thing, I've got more than enough money. Just do what makes you happy, and please, for fuck's sake, tell me that being with me is one of those things."

"Being with you is definitely one of those things."

I grinned, cupped her cheeks in my hands and kissed her; a couple of people in the kitchen cheering. She kissed me back, laughing when we broke apart.

"I just got flour all over your shirt, sorry about that."

"I don't care. Cover me in flour if you want, as long as you love me back."

She smiled up at me sweetly. "I do love you back."

"I don't suppose you get off work anytime soon?" I murmured against her lips.

"Not until after dinner. I'm counting the days until I don't have to be here from sunup past sunrise."

"Come to my house when you get off. I want to show it to you. I'll make you dinner."

She arched a brow, surprised. "Oh, you will?"

I grinned. "With an assist by my mom."

"You don't have to do that."

"I want to. You deserve the world, Shea. I want to show you how great it feels to be cared for. The way you make me and my kids feel."

"Okay, don't make me cry," she said. "You won me over already. No need to make me weepy."

I kissed her again. "I guess I should let you get back to whatever you're working on."

"Chicken potpie."

"So I'll see you tonight?"

She nodded, her eyes bright with happiness.

"I can't wait," I said, wishing I didn't have to leave.

At least we wouldn't be apart for long. I had a lot of lost time to make up for, and I could hardly wait to get started.

CHAPTER TWENTY-FOUR

Shea

ONE MONTH LATER

"Change two teaspoons of brown sugar to three," I said after tasting the butter sauce I was trying to perfect.

"Two to three. Check."

Holt stood next to the stove, a clipboard in hand, as he took the recipe notes I needed to get my cheese ravioli with butter sauce recipe just right.

Before I'd even finished working out my two-week notice at The Sleepy Moose, Holt had come up with an idea I was excited about: teaching cooking classes. He'd found and bought a downtown building that had been vacant for a couple of years and was planning to oversee its renovation.

I had plans to teach kids' classes, host themed cooking parties and teach aspiring cooks how to make staple recipes. And the best part was that with the business plan Holt had created for me, he'd shown me that I could afford to bring Nina with me.

Somehow, he'd convinced Keller to partner with him financially on this venture, even though Keller was still disappointed I'd turned him down.

"What does this need?" I asked myself out loud.

"It's usually salt," Holt answered for me.

He'd been my sous-chef of sorts all week, taking notes and making quick runs to the grocery store for more ingredients when I needed them. And, of course, taste testing. He and the kids were all over that job.

"My salt is good and I don't want garlic or lemon juice in this. I think we need to see how it tastes with the ravioli."

I plated four servings of the cheese ravioli I'd made this morning and topped each with some sauce.

"Kids, time for a taste test!" Holt called out.

Spencer and Marley came running and we all stood at the kitchen counter with our dishes, Holt counting down until we could all take our first bite, which had become our tradition this week.

"Three...two...one...go for it."

Marley nodded enthusiastically. "I love this."

"What do you love about it?" I asked her.

"The ravioli and the sauce."

I exchanged an amused look with Holt. The kids said they loved everything I made and never said anything critical. They liked feeling like a part of creating recipes, though.

"I like the sauce because it tastes really good," Spencer said. "Can I eat all of this?"

"Absolutely, eat up. Do you want more sauce?"

He nodded and said, "Yes, please."

"Who's willing to try some roasted walnuts on theirs?" I asked.

The kids preferred it without the nuts and Holt and I preferred it with. Holt made notes on his paper and the kids went back to the theater room to watch their movie.

As soon as they were out of earshot, he gave me a knowing smile.

"Already knew you wanted the nuts before you even tasted it."

My cheeks warmed as I moved my plate of unfinished ravioli over by the sink. School would be starting in a week, so the kids had been having a lot of sleepovers with their grandparents in the month Holt and I had been together.

That meant we'd been having a lot of sleepovers, too. We couldn't get enough of each other.

His years of traveling for hockey had conditioned Holt to wake up early every morning, no matter what time he'd gone to bed. Every morning that we woke up alone at his house, we went out to the deck and watched the sunrise together, then showered together and made breakfast.

I'd finally reached a point where my hips and legs didn't ache with soreness all the time from all the sex we had. He was a rock star in bed, teaching me things about my own body I never would have known.

"Is it okay if I invite Grady and Avon over for dinner tonight?" I asked him. "I want to try out a couple of pasta recipes."

"Of course. Need me to make a run to the store?"

"If you don't mind."

He came over and kissed me. "I never mind."

I smiled up at him, hoping I'd always get the butterflies I did when he looked at me this way.

"I was also thinking I might do that sleepover with Marley tonight. In the castle."

He gave me an apologetic look. "I don't want you sleeping on the floor, babe."

"I don't mind. When I had time for camping, I slept on the ground."

"She'll be really excited. And you can always sneak out once she's asleep."

I shrugged. "No reason to. There's nothing else to see or do in this house."

"Oh really?" His eyes sparkled with amusement as he wrapped his arms around my waist, squeezing my ass. "I'll give you eight inches of something to do. How about that?"

He wasn't exaggerating. I truly was the luckiest woman in the Beard.

———

"I could eat this every day," Avon said, scooping up another bite of creamed tortellini.

"Yeah, it's really good," Grady agreed.

"Thanks. You don't mind the spinach?"

Grady side-eyed his wife. "She's got me eating spinach every other night at home. I had to accept it or starve."

I laughed, remembering how much my brother had always hated spinach.

"Good for you," I said to Avon. "Spinach is so healthy, and it has a great depth of flavor."

"Avon, do you want to come to our sleepover tonight?" Marley asked.

"Me?" Avon smiled. "I would be delighted to come, thank you."

Marley sent me a gap-toothed smile. "It's in my castle."

"Nice. We're all queens who belong in castles anyway."

"Uh, the castle is for reading and you'll be sleeping on the floor," Holt said.

Marley rolled her eyes. "There are lots of pillows in there, Daddy."

I hid my smile. Marley had opened up to me a lot in the past month, and I wasn't going to turn down any invitation she offered me.

"You want to watch the game tonight?" Holt asked Grady.

"Sure. I'll have to go home to let the dog out at some point."

My brother had come a long way in the past month, too. He initially wanted to fight Holt for being in a relationship with me, which was absurd but also classic Ryan Grady. Slowly, though, he'd lightened up after spending time with the two of us and the kids.

"Okay, it's time for linguini with vodka sauce," I said, standing up.

"Let me just loosen my belt first," Grady grumbled. "I just ate an entire plate of the tortellini."

"Which I told you not to do because there was another pasta to try," I reminded him.

"I couldn't help it. It was good."

Holt helped me clear dishes and plate the linguine.

"Let me grate some parm for this real quick," I said, walking over to the fridge.

These days, I knew this kitchen better than my own. Holt's builder had created a perfect space for a gourmet, with top-of-the-line appliances and lots of little touches like a pot filler and a warming drawer.

"So Holt, how are you keeping from gaining a ton of weight with Shea cooking for you every day?" Avon asked. "I think I'd just give in and buy elastic waistband pants."

He chuckled. "I had to up the distance of my morning run, but it's so worth it."

I brought over a block of parmesan cheese and Holt was waiting with the grater. "I've got the grating. You just put it on like you want it."

I sprinkled grated cheese on each plate of pasta and Spencer delivered the plates to the table.

"This would be a good time to be a cow," Grady told Spencer.

"So you could have milk?" Spencer asked.

"No, because they have more than one stomach."

"Oh, get off it," I said to my brother. "You eat more than anyone I know."

"I'm a growing boy," he said, shrugging.

"You're right about the boy part."

We all sat down and Holt did the countdown to our first bite. The vodka sauce I'd made had some spice, but the kids both ate it without complaint.

"It's divine," Avon said.

"I was thinking of maybe adding some sausage?" I said.

"I think I'd like it better with meat," Holt said. "Sausage would be good."

"It tastes like tomatoes," Marley said, wrinkling her nose and setting her fork down.

The kids snuck away from the table as soon as they could, going outside to play on the huge play set with swings, slides and a climbing wall. The adults stayed in for after-dinner drinks, the men doing the cleanup while Avon and I sat out on the deck.

"So how's married life?" I asked her.

"Honestly, it's not that much different than life before we were married. But I do love hearing him call me his wife."

"He's so happy."

She smiled, a dreamy look in her eyes. "So am I."

It was starting to get cooler, especially in the

evenings and mornings. I loved sitting on the deck with a sweater on, watching the sun slip below the horizon. Once I opened my business, I'd have to work some evenings, but I planned to work a lot less than I had at The Sleepy Moose. There were only so many sunsets in life, and I wanted to watch as many of them as I could with people I loved.

"Holt is so completely gone for you," Avon said with a grin. "He looks at you like you hung the moon."

"I feel the same way about him. I keep waiting for the honeymoon phase to wear off, but it just doesn't. Every time I get a text from him or pull into his driveway, I'm just so damn happy."

"You deserve it. Both of you do. Have there been any more issues with his ex?"

I shook my head. "He hasn't heard from her since she came to town and he shut her down."

"Good." She glanced over at the kids on the play set. "They seem really happy and settled here."

"I think they are. They're excited about starting school."

She gave me a knowing look. "I foresee a lot of nooners in your future."

"Oh, for sure. Holt is all over it."

"And you'll be able to set your own hours. I'm so

damn happy you're not at The Moose for twelve hours a day anymore."

My sister-in-law finished her wine and stood up. "I'm going for a refill. Let me top you off while I'm in there."

"Thanks."

I passed her my glass and took the moment of solitude to look out at the lake's gently lapping waves. It was so good to live life slowly sometimes. To soak up the small things like a delicious glass of wine and a sunset painted with shades of orange and pink.

Knowing what it was like to live full speed ahead all the time made me appreciate these moments more. Never again would I spend more time at work than at home.

It was the first time I'd ever felt more excited about the future of my personal life than work. It was true what they said about finding the person you wanted to spend the rest of your life with making you want it to start as soon as possible.

I wouldn't take a single moment with Holt, Spencer and Marley for granted.

CHAPTER TWENTY-FIVE

Holt

ONE YEAR LATER

"Another game, another win for the Sven's Beard Squatches!" I pumped my fist in celebration with Spencer's team, which was my favorite to coach for obvious reasons.

Though Spence hadn't been interested in playing hockey when we lived in Minneapolis, he wanted to play when he found out all his friends at school did.

Spending time at the arena teaching him the game I loved was a dream come true for me. Grady coached Marley's team, but I joined him for as many practices and games as I could. Hockey was a way of life in the Beard, and I loved that my kids had embraced it.

"Spence, did your mom make snacks?" one of his teammates asked him as we gathered our gear at the bench.

"Yeah, she made ice cream bars," Spencer said, clearly pleased.

Other kids assumed Shea was my kids' mom since she was at every practice and game and also at our house every time anyone came over. After hiring someone to care for the yard at the home she was rarely at all summer, I'd finally convinced her to move in.

I'd always thought I was too traditional to have a woman living in my home with me and my kids when we weren't married, but the four of us had been going to counseling to make sure we made the best choices for the kids, and our therapist had opened our eyes to a few things.

Being a family wasn't about technicalities like a marriage license. It was about being there for each other through the good times and the bad. The kids and I wanted Shea to officially move in, and I planned to propose to her within the next year.

Everything we wanted, we already had. Marrying her would make it official, and I wanted that, too, but for now, the kids needed to get used to her living with us.

The boys dumped their sweaty hockey gear in the locker room and showered, cleaning the mess up quickly because they knew Shea's homemade ice cream bars were waiting.

It took her a long time to make them, but they were always a huge hit with the kids. She wrapped each bar in paper stamped with "Sven's Kitchen," the name of her business.

When we met up with her in the snack bar, Spencer ran into her arms for a congratulatory hug.

"Did you see my assist?" he asked her.

"Of course I did. Great job!"

Avon stood near our table, five-week-old Georgie in her arms. She and Grady were over the moon excited about their new daughter. Grady was itching to take her around the rink for a skate in her daddy's arms, but Avon refused to let him until she was older.

"Ice cream bar?" Shea asked me, holding one out.

"You know it. Thanks, babe."

I opened it and took a bite, finding a layer of caramel in the center of the chocolate-coated home-made vanilla ice cream on a stick.

"You added caramel," I said. "It's amazing."

"I thought you might like it."

Now that I was skating a lot and getting into the weight room with my teams, I was back in fighting form. I'd put on around fifteen happy pounds over the first few months of my relationship with Shea.

Grady walked into the snack bar, a giant in his ice skates with guards. He immediately made an overly happy face for Georgie, his mouth open and his eyes wide.

"There's my future Olympic hockey champion," he said, opening his arms. "Come see Daddy."

"Did you wash your hands?" Avon asked.

"Yes, warden."

She gave him a look and Grady kissed her before she passed him the baby.

"There she is," he said, kissing her forehead and cradling her. "My perfect little Gigi."

Georgie made a face and grunted, Grady's expression shifting.

"And she just had a diaper blowout."

He looked at his wife, who passed him the diaper bag. "I'm sure it's a perfect little explosion meant just for her dad."

Grady shook his head and looked at me. "Will you help? It takes me like thirty-five wipes to change a poopy diaper."

"Absolutely not."

"Really? You're afraid of a tiny little baby's poop?"

I shrugged. "I wouldn't call it fear. Better get to it, sometimes it leaks through their diapers and then you have a much worse mess on your hands."

"I'm just gonna go hold her under a cool shower."

I shook my head. "Not happening. That's a health hazard."

"Ryan Grady, go change your daughter's diaper," Avon said.

He put the strap of the diaper bag over his shoulder and walked away with a reluctant expression.

"I bet he's going to go call Mom," Shea quipped. "For real. And she'd come running."

Avon laughed. "It's true. Did I tell you she cried the first time she fed Georgie? She is so in love with that little girl."

"You'll never be without a babysitter," Shea said. "If you call her at two a.m., she'll be there."

Shea's parents treated Spencer and Marley like grandchildren already. My kids had lost people from their lives, but they'd gained more. They'd spent two weeks with their mom over the summer, and I'd worried every minute of it that she'd try to leave the country with them.

No one but Shea would ever know that I'd told Andrea I'd pay her twenty thousand dollars when I picked the kids up from her. It was my insurance that they'd be there, and I planned to pay it every summer.

"Hey, I have to go warm up the peewee team," I said to Shea. "I'll be out of here by five."

"Okay, I'm going home to let Muffin out and then I'll be back. You still good grilling for dinner?"

"Yep. I've got dinner covered, babe."

I kissed her and took Spencer with me to be a water boy for the next game. Marley was hanging out with some of her teammates, their game already over, and I knew she'd want to go with Shea to let our eight-month-old golden retriever out.

His name was Blueberry Muffin Sellers—Muffin for short. The four of us had all put a name on a piece of paper and Marley's had been the one drawn.

But even with a male dog named Muffin, life was just about perfect. My life had been leveled by my divorce, but I'd rebuilt it with care, and it showed.

I thought I had it all when I was a pro hockey player, but I'd been so wrong. This was the first time in my life I had everything that mattered, and I cherished it every single day.

ALSO BY BRENDA ROTHERT

CHICAGO BLAZE SERIES

Book 1 - Anton

Book 2 - Luca

Book 3 - Victor

Book 4 - Knox

Book 5 - Alexei

Book 6 - Easy

Book 7 - Jonah

Book 8 - Kit

Book 9 - Olivier

COLORADO COYOTES SERIES

Book 1 - The Donor

Book 2 - The Opponent

SIN CITY SAINTS SERIES

Book 1 - Maverick

Book 2 - Pike

Book 3 - Pax

ST. LOUS MAVERICKS SERIES

Book 1 - Hard Fall

Book 2 - Hard Limit

Book 3 - Hard Pass

Book 4 - Hard Luck

FIRE ON ICE SERIES

Book 1 - Bound

Book 2 - Captive

Book 3 - Edge

Book 4 - Drive

Book 5 - Release

ON THE LINE SERIES

Book 1 - Killian

Book 2 - Bennett

LOCKHART BROTHERS SERIES

Book 1 - Deep Down

Book 2 - In Deep

Book 3 - Drawn Deeper

Book 4 - Hidden Depth

FILTHY SERIES

Book 1 - Dirty Work

Book 2 - Dirty Secret

Book 3 - Dirty Defiance

ABOUT THE AUTHOR

Brenda Rothert lives in Central Illinois with her husband, children and dogs. A former print journalist, she has written more than fifty romance novels. Her print and e-books have been translated into German, Italian and Portuguese, and her audiobooks have been translated into German.

She loves to hear from readers through her website or her Facebook Group, Rothert's Readers.

www.ingramcontent.com/pod-product-compliance
Lightning Source LLC
Chambersburg PA
CBHW011852300726
48970CB00009B/2760